Spring Tinderbox

Festivals, poems, stories, songs and activities

Compiled by Chris Deshpande and Julia Eccleshare

A & C Black · London

Contents

First published 1992 by A & C Black Ltd
35 Bedford Row, London WC1R 4JH

Text © 1992 A & C Black Ltd
Inside illustrations © 1992 David Price
Cover illustration by Alex Ayliffe
Edited by Jill Brand
Designed by Janet Watson

Photoset by Rowland Phototypesetting Ltd,
Bury St Edmunds, Suffolk
Printed in Great Britain by
St Edmundsbury Press Ltd, Bury St Edmunds, Suffolk

ISBN 0-7136-3660-2

The arrival of spring

Winter's end

It was deep winter. The land lay covered with snow and even the swift stream had frozen hard. The old man huddled over his dying fire, shivering. He longed to hear a human voice once more before death came for him, but the only sound in his lonely valley was that of the wind in the trees.

Then, one morning, a fine young man came to his hut. He strode along with a light step, singing a happy song. In his hand he bore not a spear but a spray of fresh flowers.

'Come in, my son,' said the old man. 'It is many days since I last heard the sound of a voice, and I am right glad to see you. Sit down. You shall tell me all about your travels and the strange adventures you have had, and I will tell you what I have been doing, too.'

The young man flung himself down beside the fire and they settled comfortably to talk.

'First,' said the old man, 'I shall tell what powers I have. When I send out my breath the waters stand still. They become like stone.'

'When I breathe out,' said the young man, 'flowers spring up all over the meadow.'

'I shake my hair,' said the old man, 'and snow falls from the sky and covers the whole land. I speak and the leaves fall. Birds fly away and every animal hides from my sight, I tread on the ground and it becomes rock-hard.'

'I shake my long hair,' said the young man, 'and soft rain drops out of the sky and waters the earth. Plants peep out of the ground like children searching for their mothers. I sing and birds return from their homes in distant lands. I breathe over the waters and they flow again. When I walk through the woods all nature sings to greet me.'

They fell silent and sat there, both staring at the flickering flames of the dying fire. The sun had broken through the clouds and the air in the clearing suddenly felt quite warm. A songbird began to trill from the roof. There was a soft murmur as the frozen stream began to flow again. A light breeze arose, full of the scent of newly-opened flowers.

The young man stretched his limbs and smiled in the sunshine. He turned to look at his companion. The old man was lying limply beside the fire. His face had fallen in, and moisture was flowing from his eyes. As the strength of the sun grew, he seemed to shrink, until by noonday he had quite vanished, leaving only a puddle of water which quickly turned to vapour.

Where the old man had been sitting, a tiny plant sprang out of the ground. It had a delicate white and pink flower, the first herald of spring.

Marcus Crouch

Spring

Sound the flute!
Now it's mute:
Birds delight
Day and night,
Nightingale
In the dale,
Lark in sky –
Merrily
Merrily, merrily to welcome in the year.

Little Boy,
Full of joy;
Little Girl,
Sweet and small;
Cock does crow,
So do you;
Merry voice,
Infant noise,
Merrily, merrily to welcome in the year.

William Blake

Over

Spring is overrated
Summer is overheated
Autumn is overwritten
Winter is overthankgod.

Roger McGough

At long last, spring has arrived!

At long last, spring has arrived.
'So there you are!' I said icily.
'About time too!' I said frostily.
'You're late!' I said coldly.

'Cool it,' she said mildly.
'I've been under a lot of pressure lately.
Have a daffodil.'

'Blooming cheek,' I said,
In the heat of the moment.

Colin McNaughton

There goes Winter

Look at red-faced Winter
Slouching down the road,
Coughing and puffing
In his tatty grey overcoat and scarf,
Dew-drop on the end of his nose!

See his frosty breath
Turn the rain white and fragile,
Stiffen pond and puddle,
Make ground tight-fisted,
Spike the eaves with icicles!

Listen how he brings
Shivers and shudders,
Grumbles and groans
To pavements and roadways,
Car-parks and playgrounds!

Old dawdler!

But wait, watch him shuffle away
Over the hill
Into a green dream
Of snowdrop and crocus coming our way!

Matt Simpson

from The Selfish Giant

This is a story about a giant, who had a very beautiful garden, and about the consequences of his selfish behaviour. The giant went to visit a friend and stayed with him for seven years. While he was away all the children from the neighbourhood would play in his garden. On his return home the giant was very angry and banned them from the garden. He put up a high wall and a sign which read 'TRESPASSERS WILL BE PROSECUTED!' This not only stopped the children from playing in the garden but also stopped Spring from entering.

Then the Spring came, and all over the country there were little blossoms and little birds. Only in the garden of the Selfish Giant it was still winter. The birds did not care to sing in it as there were no children, and the trees forgot to blossom. Once a beautiful flower put its head out from the grass, but when it saw the notice-board it was so sorry for the children that it slipped back into the ground again, and went off to sleep. The only people who were pleased were the Snow and the Frost. 'Spring has forgotten this garden,' they cried, 'so we will live here all the year round.' The Snow covered up the grass with her great white cloak, and the Frost painted all the trees silver. Then they invited the North Wind to stay with them, and he came. He was wrapped in furs, and he roared all day about the garden, and blew the chimney-pots down. 'This is a delightful spot,' he said, 'we must ask the Hail on a visit.' So the Hail came. Every day for three hours he rattled on the roof of the castle till he broke most of the slates, and then he ran round and round the garden as fast as he could go. He was dressed in grey, and his breath was like ice.

'I cannot understand why Spring is so late in coming,' said the Selfish Giant as he sat at the window and looked out at his cold white garden; 'I hope there will be a change in the weather.'

But the Spring never came, nor the Summer. The Autumn gave golden fruit to every garden, but to the Giant's garden she gave none. 'He is too selfish,' she said. So it was always winter there, and the North Wind and the Hail, and the Frost, and the Snow danced about through the trees.

One morning the Giant was lying awake in bed when he heard some lovely music. It sounded so sweet to his ears that he thought it must be the King's musicians passing by. It was really only a little linnet singing outside his window, but it was so long since he had heard a bird sing in his garden that it seemed to him to be the most beautiful music in the world. Then the Hail stopped dancing over his head, and the North Wind ceased roaring, and a delicious perfume came to him through the open casement. 'I believe the Spring has come at last,' said the Giant; and he jumped out of bed and looked out.

What did he see?

He saw a most wonderful sight. Through a little hole in the wall the children had crept in, and they were sitting in the branches of the trees. In every tree that he could see there was a little child. And the trees were so glad to have the children back again that they had covered themselves with blossoms, and were waving their arms gently above the children's heads. The birds were flying about and twittering with delight, and the flowers were looking up through the green grass and laughing. It was a lovely scene, only in one corner it was still winter. It was the farthest corner of the garden, and in it was standing a little boy. He was so small that he could not reach up to the branches of the tree, and he was wandering all round it crying bitterly. The poor tree was still quite covered with frost and snow, and the North Wind was blowing and roaring above it. 'Climb up! little boy,' said the Tree, and it bent its branches down as low as it could, but the boy was too tiny.

And the Giant's heart melted as he looked out. 'How selfish I have been!' he said; 'Now I know why the Spring would not come here. I will put that poor little boy on the top of the tree, and then I will knock down the wall, and my garden shall be the children's playground for ever and ever.' He was really very sorry for what he had done.

Oscar Wilde

THE SEASONS

Before they had clocks and calendars people marked the passing of time by the length of the light and darkness of each day. The sun and the moon were the first clocks and the rhythm of the sun and moon were the first calendars. The seasons were times of warmth and cold.

Equinoxes occur twice a year when the sun is directly over the equator and the hours of daylight exactly equal the hours of darkness. The spring equinox is the 21st March and the autumn equinox is 22nd September.

The seasons occur because the earth rotates around the sun at an angle, making each hemisphere alternately nearer or further away from it. In the northern hemisphere spring occurs in the early months of the year, and in the southern hemisphere it occurs in the latter part of the year. Parts of the world with a tropical climate have only two seasons, wet (rainy) and dry.

CALENDARS

Different cultures have found different ways of measuring the passage of time. The Jewish, Islamic and Hindu traditions, for example, use a lunar calendar, based on the time it takes for the moon to orbit the earth.

Solar calendars, like the Baha'i and Gregorian ones, are based on the length of time it takes the earth to orbit the sun. The Gregorian calendar is the one which is used mainly by the countries of the West and in Japan. It was pre-dated by the Julian calendar which was introduced by Julius Caesar in 46 BC. The Julian calendar is still used by the eastern Orthodox churches in Greece and Rumania to calculate the date of Easter.

The Gregorian calendar was introduced by Pope Gregory XIII in 1582, but the British Parliament did not officially accept it until 1752. By this time Britain had fallen 11 days behind the countries who had adopted it earlier. When the change took place, the days between 2nd and 14th September were dropped. The decision led to rioting in the streets by people who thought they had been robbed of 11 days of their lives.

FLORAL CALENDARS

In about 2000 BC the Chinese Goddess of Flowers, Ho-Hsien-Ku, announced that a different flower for each month of the year would be honoured and respected.

January	Plum blossom
February	Peach blossom
March	Tree peony
April	Cherry blossom
May	Magnolia
June	Pomegranate
July	Lotus
August	Pear blossom
September	Mallow
October	Chrysanthemum
November	Gardenia
December	Poppy

Other cultures also have floral calendars, the Japanese one being very similar to the Chinese. The English floral calendar names a flower for each month and also gives it a symbolic meaning. The spring months are like this:

March	Daffodil	Self-love
April	Daisy	Innocence
May	Lily of the valley	Return of happiness
June	Rose	Love

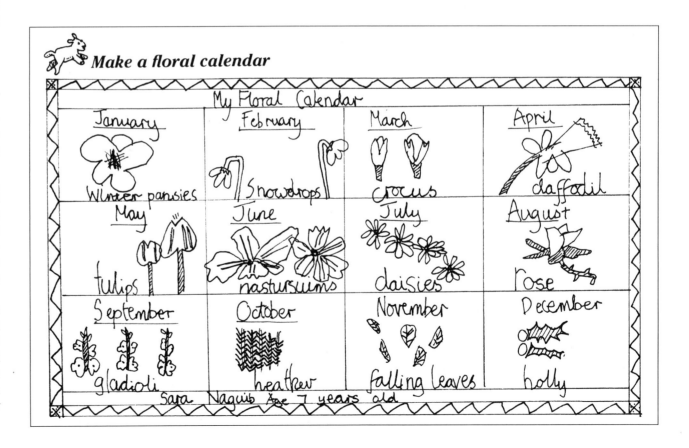

Make a floral calendar

My Floral Calendar

January — Winter pansies
February — Snowdrops
March — crocus
April — daffodil
May — tulips
June — nasturtiums
July — daisies
August — rose
September — gladioli
October — heather
November — falling leaves
December — holly

Sara Naguib age 7 years old

Cuckoo Fair

One April evening long ago, old Mother Merriweather stood in her cottage porch muttering and peering into the chilly green twilight. Her old brown hands, wrinkled and gnarled as the apple trees in her garden, wove wheedling, beckoning signs towards the darkening sky.

'Come on! Come on!' she murmured. 'You be late, m'dear! Where be you m'liddle dear?'

At her feet lay a big market basket of brown eggs, yellow butter-pats and round cheeses.

'There be jest room fer you m'dear. Come! Come! Come!'

So, muttering and beckoning, she scanned the sky with her old eyes until at last she spied a tiny speck in the silver mists that lay above the dark forests of the Weald. The speck grew and grew, took bird shape, flew nearer and nearer, until it sank with softly fluttering wings into old Mother Merriweather's market basket.

She grinned toothlessly down at the small bird with dark silver bars on its white breast.

'So you be come, m'dear,' she crooned. 'And summer be come wi' you.'

She tied a snowy cloth over the basket, and left it in the porch when she hobbled up to bed. Tomorrow was April the fourteenth and she must be up at dawn to take the cuckoo to Heathfield Fair. There she would let him fly away and when the good folk of Sussex heard his song they would rejoice, knowing that summer had come.

'My bit o' magic!' she whispered happily as she pulled the bed covers up to her chin. 'My own lovely bit o' magic! Nubuddy but me can call the cuckoo, and nubuddy but me can let him fly. THEY gave the gift to old Mother Merriweather ages long agone . . . beyond the

mists of time . . . beyond the mists of time.' Smiling, the old woman slept.

Now, in the cottage next door lived old Gaffer Winterthorne, a meddlesome, mischief-making old fellow who never could mind his own business. He was peeping from his kitchen window when old Mother Merriweather was making her good magic, and he chuckled nastily into his whiskers.

'Lot o' nonsense this be,' he scoffed. 'Why should her be in charge o' the cuckoo? Now, what can I do to upset things, hey?'

He sat thinking for a long time. He was still there at midnight when the painted wooden cuckoo in his clock on the wall popped out and called 'Cuckoo' twelve times. Old Gaffer Winterthorne thumped the table. 'Ha! Got it!' he cried. 'I'll have a real live cuckoo in my clock instead of a toy one, and I'll make old Mother Merriweather look a proper cuckoo herself when she opens her basket at Cuckoo Fair.'

Thereupon he took the wooden cuckoo out of the clock and hurried with it round to his neighbour's porch. The stars winked reproachfully as he lifted a corner of the cloth and took from the basket the lovely living bird. Its feathers were soft and warm, and its tiny heart beat fast under his clumsy hand. He left the painted wooden cuckoo in the basket and hurried home. He chuckled to think what a very clever thing he had done as he popped the live bird into his clock and closed the tiny door.

'A real cuckoo clock I have, now,' he said. 'And how the folk will mock old Mother Merriweather come morn!'

Old Mother Merriweather was up betimes and off to the Fair, her basket on her arm. A chattering crowd quickly gathered.

'It's old Mother Merriweather – watch out children, and see the cuckoo fly!'

Old Mother Merriweather bent and whisked away the cloth. But no cuckoo flew joyfully upwards. Only a stupid wooden bird gazed up with painted eyes.

'Aw!' and 'Ooh!' and 'Aah!' sighed the people. 'Old Mother Merriweather has lost her magic powers!' Some laughed and pointed scornfully, but most wept because the cuckoo had not come, and there would be no summer that year.

Old Mother Merriweather stared down at the wooden cuckoo and she burst into tears. 'Oh my! Oh my!' she sobbed, 'Whatever can ha' happened?' But she soon understood and was very angry indeed.

'It's that old Gaffer Winterthorne,' she stormed to herself, 'I know him and his tricks.'

She unloaded her eggs and butter and cheeses on to the nearest stall, and taking up her basket she hurried home.

Breathless and red in the face she hobbled up old Gaffer Winterthorne's garden path and banged on his door. He opened his lattice window.

'Be you after summat?' he asked innocently.

'After summat?' the old woman raged. 'You know full well what I'm after. What ha' you done wi' my cuckoo?'

The old man slammed his window shut.

Old Mother Merriweather stooped to the keyhole of his door and cried, 'If cuckoo don't fly, summer won't come!'

Old Gaffer Winterthorne did not answer.

'And if summer don't come your beans and peas and taters won't grow!' she added.

The old man began to doubt if he had been so very clever after all.

'And there'll be no flowers, and the bees won't make honey, and I'll tell everyone whose fault it is. They'll be after you, surely, you see if they ain't!' old Mother Merriweather went on, kicking the door.

Old Gaffer Winterthorne kept silent, but he trembled a little.

Then the old woman screamed, 'If you got my cuckoo in your clock you're a proper daft old man, I reckon. He'll never call cuckoo while he be shut in a clock. He'll jest mope and die!'

Old Gaffer Winterthorne's jaw dropped open. Now that he came to think about it he realised the cuckoo had made no sound since he put it in the clock.

He jumped up and opened the little door. Sure enough, the poor bird sat with drooping wings and hooded eyes. He snatched it from the clock, opened his front door, and thrust the dying bird at the old woman.

'Here, take your old cuckoo,' he said. 'He be nigh dead, I reckon, like you said. Give me my lovely painted wooden bird!'

Old Mother Merriweather flung the wooden cuckoo at him and seized her darling bird. She stroked its feathers and whispered words of love. She wove her good magic over it, and its wings began to flutter. Then she put it in her basket and hurried back to the Fair.

Once more the people gathered. Old Mother Merriweather beamed round at them. She stooped and whisked the cloth from her basket. Up flew the cuckoo, joyous and free, away into the blue. It sang 'Cuckoo, cuckoo, cuckoo,' and the people cheered and threw their hats in the air, and all over Sussex they danced for joy that summer had come.

Ruth C Paine

The fight of the year

And there goes the bell for the third month and
winter comes out of its corner
looking groggy
Spring leads with a left to the head
followed by a sharp right to the body
   daffodils
   primroses
   crocuses
   snowdrops
   lilacs
   violets
   pussywillow
Winter can't take much more punishment
and Spring shows no sign of tiring
   tadpoles
   squirrels
   baalambs
   badgers
   bunny rabbits
   mad March hares
   horses and hounds

Spring is merciless
Winter won't go the full twelve rounds
   bobtail clouds
   scallywag winds
   the sun
   a pavement artist
   in every town
A left to the chin
and Winter's down!
   tomatoes
   radish
   cucumber
   onions
   beetroot
   celery
   and any
   amount
   of lettuce
   for dinner
Winter's out for the count
Spring is the winner!

Roger McGough

 Using the poem

The poet uses a combative style to introduce the oncoming of spring, listing the strengths of the season. A defence of winter could be made with the class making a list of positive aspects of winter. This might include snow, snowmen, snowball fights, sledging and skiing, being able to see the stars and moon because of the earlier nights, robins, Guy Fawkes night, garden bonfires, fewer flies, no stinging insects . . .

This could lead on to a debate – winter against spring. A group representing each season could choose to be characters associated with their particular season, for example, Jack Frost and Babushka or the mad March hare and the Easter bunny. The rest of the class would listen to the arguments and then vote to see if spring really is the winner as suggested by the poet.

THE SIGNS OF SPRING

There is a 19th century proverb which says that spring has arrived when you can tread on nine daisies at the same time. One doesn't have to wait for the daisies to have the arrival of spring confirmed. There are many signs which children can observe both in rural and urban settings.

Spring is the time when plants and trees start to show signs of growth. The primrose (meaning the first rose), the crocus, catkin and coltsfoot are early flowers and many trees start to bud.

The dawn chorus of birds, particularly blackbirds and song thrushes, heralds the onset of spring. Many small creatures start to appear. Worms, slugs and snails will emerge in search of food, leaving a thin, sticky trail behind them. These trails are easily seen on concrete paths and walls.

In early spring queen bumble bees can be spotted as they search for a place to start a new nest. They first feed off the early spring flowers to give them strength after the winter hibernation. The honey bee will be out as soon as the day temperatures rise, along with early butterflies such as the brimstone, peacock and tortoise-shell.

A pond starts to come to life in early spring. Frogs and toads waking up after the winter's hibernation head to the pond to spawn. Many water insects are now in evidence.

Recording signs of spring

There are many activities which will help develop children's observation and recording skills and which will heighten their awareness of the onset of the spring.

1. To study the mini-world of a pond a pond-dipping expedition can be an invaluable source of specimens to study at close hand. Remember to take great care when near water and to replace all specimens before leaving. (Advice about collecting and rearing frogspawn is on page 33.) The children can make detailed sketches and log all the information needed before leaving. If possible, more than one visit to the pond should be made so the children can observe the changes in pond life as they occur. Cross-sectional models of the pond with three-dimensional models of the creatures and plants of the pond can be made to enhance the factual study.

2. A flower or plant diary is a way of noting the first appearance of plants. A study of the streets and grass verges around the school or home can be very enlightening. City streets may seem bare but many different types of plants grow unnoticed between paving stones and by walls. The children can be given different types of area to watch and notes can be compared.

If there is some waste land nearby the class could 'adopt' it as a wildlife area and keep a running record of the changes it goes through during the season. If a photographic record is kept it is a good idea to include a card clearly showing the date in each photograph.

A plan of the area can be drawn on which children plot where different plants and flowers were found, along with the date. Some plants could be measured regularly and their rates of growth charted. The class could plant wild flower seeds onto the land to increase the variety of flowers. Wildlife that inhabits the areas can be investigated and recorded separately or included on the same map.

3. A study of a wall can also be very informative. It may appear that there is nothing on the wall, but on closer inspection a mini-world can be discovered. The older the wall the more life it supports. In early spring plants will start to grow in the crevices and, on damp walls, mosses and ferns will start to unfurl. Insects and small creatures such as slugs, snails, woodlice, wolf spiders and early butterflies can often be found.

You could make a large frieze of the wall and, each time a different life-form is discovered, a group of children could find out all they can about it and then make a model or picture to be added to the wall. The study of the wall could have a time limit of a day, a week or a month. A record of the stages of the life-form, where and when it was discovered, and how long it stayed on the wall, can be made.

Could this be a sign?

No scarves around us,
Could this be a sign?
No hats upon our heads,
Could this be a sign?
    Spring is here!
    It's peeping through the sky;
      Goodbye, goodbye,
      Goodbye, winter time.

Buds have grown on every tree,
Could this be a sign?
The frost has gone and the grass is green,
Could this be a sign?
    Spring is here . . .

Watching birds as they make their nests,
Could this be a sign?
They work and sing and they never rest,
Could this be a sign?
    Spring is here . . .

Yellow streams of daffodils,
Could this be a sign?
Cuckoo calling from the gill,
Could this be a sign?
    Spring is here . . .

New born lambs skipping in the fields,
Could this be a sign?
Cows are grazing a grassy meal,
Could this be a sign?
    Spring is here . . .

Words and music by Niki Davies

The world in springtime

A poem with knickers in it

It's getting spring
In Holland Park
Trees brazen it out.

Daffodils in a heap
Around their ankles
Like frilly yellow knickers.

Roger McGough

Spring

The grey snow's melting: tricklings going on
in gutters and in grids. The grass is back.
The year is perking up again and gardens now
are thinking of getting glad-rags on,
bringing crocus, primrose, daffodil out of
the dark wardrobe. The avenues will want
to show off their cherry blossom soon
like posh weddings, and the hawthorn
will smell as sweet as marzipan again
where the thrushes hide their Easter eggs.

Matt Simpson

The spring months

March brings breezes loud and shrill,
Stirs the dancing daffodil.

April brings the primrose sweet,
Scatters daisies at our feet.

May brings flocks of pretty lambs,
Skipping by their fleecy dams.

Sara Coleridge
from The months of the year

Spring in the city

Spring has come to the city,
to the streets and the railway line,
winter is packing its bags,
the sun has begun to shine.

I hear the babble of birdsong,
and the calls of the geese in flight,
trees are in bud once more
and the days are warm with delight.

A heron is raising its young
at the flooded gravel pits,
and the nest box on our garden wall
is home for baby tits.

Cowslips and jack-by-the-hedge
bloom at the side of the road,
while near the pond in the city square
I discover a sleepy toad.

A blanket of yellow coltsfoot
spreads across derelict land,
while from the bridge across the lake
sparrows take bread from my hand.

Wrens are finding new homes
in an untidy overgrown hedge.
Pigeons choose a tall building
and jostle for space on a ledge.

When the city sleeps at night,
foxes are hunting again,
seeking food for their hungry cubs
that tumble and play in their den.

Spring has come to the city,
there's a lightness in everyone's tread.
Business men have shed their coats,
There's a promise of summer ahead.

Brian Moses

Three days into March

Today
the birds sang
and yellow crocuses
opened wide their mouths
to feast on sunlight.

Today
the sky cleared
and enthusiastic trees
stretched out their limbs
all thick with promises.

Today
I stood still
and the greens, the blues
and the yellows clamoured
to dance behind
my eyes.

Moira Andrew

Clearing at dawn

The fields are chill, the sparse rain has stopped;
The colours of spring teem on every side.
With leaping fish the blue pond is full;
With singing thrushes the green boughs droop.
The flowers of the field have dabbled their powdered cheeks;
The mountain grasses are bent level at the waist.
By the bamboo stream the last fragment of cloud
Blown by the wind slowly scatters away.

Li Po
Translated from the Chinese by Arthur Waley

The secret garden in spring

Mary is an orphan who has been sent to live in her uncle's huge, gloomy house on the Yorkshire moors. She is lonely and has little to amuse her, but she discovers a secret neglected garden, and also makes friends with Dickon, a local boy. He has an amazing way with animals and knows a great deal about the natural world. Together they tend the garden and Mary discovers the excitement of seeing things grow and thrive.

On that first morning when the sky was blue again, Mary wakened very early. The sun was pouring in slanting rays through the blinds and there was something so joyous in the sight of it that she jumped out of bed and ran to the window. She drew up the blinds and opened the window itself, and a great waft of fresh, scented air blew in upon her. The moor was blue and the whole world looked as if something Magic had happened to it. There were tender little fluting sounds here and there and everywhere, as if scores of birds were beginning to tune up for a concert. Mary put her hand out of the window and held it in the sun.

'It's warm – warm!' she said. 'It will make the green points push up and up and up, and it will make the bulbs and roots work and struggle with all their might under the earth.'

She kneeled down and leaned out of the window as far as she could, breathing big breaths and sniffing the air until she laughed because she remembered what Dickon's mother had said about the end of his nose quivering like a rabbit's.

'It must be very early,' she said. 'The little clouds are all pink and I've never seen the sky look like this. No one is up. I don't even hear the stable boys.'

A sudden thought made her scramble to her feet.

'I can't wait! I am going to see the garden!'

She put on her clothes in five minutes. She knew a small side door which she could unbolt herself, and she flew downstairs in her stocking feet and put her shoes on in the hall. She unchained and unbolted and unlocked, and when the door was open she sprang across the step with one bound, and there she was standing on the grass, which seemed to have turned green, and with the sun pouring down on her and warm, sweet wafts about her and the fluting and twittering and singing coming from every bush and tree. She clasped her hands for pure joy and looked up in the sky, and it was so blue and pink and pearly and white and flooded with springtime light that she felt as if she must flute and sing aloud herself, and knew that the thrushes and robins and skylarks could not possibly help it. She ran around the shrubs and paths towards the secret garden.

'It's different already,' she said. 'The grass is greener and things are sticking up everywhere and things are uncurling and the green buds of leaves are showing. This afternoon I'm sure Dickon will come.'

The long warm rain had done strange things to the herbaceous beds which bordered the walk by the lower wall. There were things sprouting and pushing out from the roots of clumps of plants and there were actually here and there glimpses of royal purple and yellow unfurling among the stems of crocuses. Six months before Mistress Mary would not have seen how the world was waking up, but now she missed nothing.

When she reached the place where the door hid itself under the ivy, she was startled by a curious loud sound. It was the caw-caw of a crow, and it came from the top of the wall, and when she looked up, there sat a big, glossy-plumaged, blue-black bird, looking down at her very wisely indeed. She had never seen a crow so close before, and he made her a little nervous, but the next moment he spread his wings and flapped away across the garden. She hoped he was not going to stay inside, and she pushed the door open wondering if he would. When she got fairly into the garden she saw that he probably did intend to stay, because he had alighted on a dwarf apple-tree, and under the apple-tree was lying a little reddish animal with a bushy tail, and both of them were watching the stooping body and rust-red head of Dickon, who was kneeling on the grass working hard.

Mary flew across the grass to him.

'Oh, Dickon! Dickon!' she cried out. 'How could you get here so early! How could you! The sun has only just got up!'

He got up himself, laughing and glowing, and tousled; his eyes like a bit of the sky.

'Eh!' he said. 'I was up long before him. How could I have stayed abed! Th' world's all fair begun again this mornin' it has. An' it's workin' an' hummin' an' scratchin' an' pipin' an' nest-buildin' an' breathin' out scents, till you've got to be out on it 'stead o' lyin' on your back. When th' sun did jump up, th' moor went mad for joy, an' I was in the midst of th' heather, an' I run like mad myself, shoutin' and singin'. An' I come straight here. I couldn't have stayed away. Why, th' garden was lyin' here waitin'!'

Frances Hodgson Burnett
from The secret garden

Spring is here

Spring is here, spring is here,
How do we know that spring is here?
The birds are singing in the trees,
Birds are singing in the trees,
That's how we know that spring is here,
That's how we know that spring is here.

Words and music by Tamar Swade

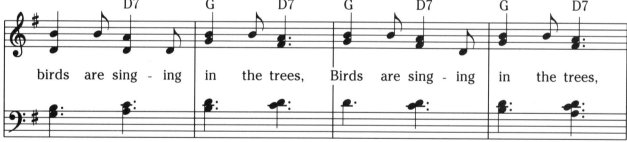

Only one verse is given here – it is a song for children to make their own by thinking of all the answers they can to the question 'How do we know that spring is here?' The answers don't need to rhyme though they do need to be worded to fit the rhythm of the middle section. Make a new verse for each different answer or accumulate them from one verse to the next.

Sounds to represent each new sign of spring can be added using improvised or classroom instruments.

New beginnings

Wumbulgal

Wumbulgal, the little duck, lived a long, long time ago in the Dream Time. She was a bold little duck who refused to be frightened by anything, even the water devil who lived in the murky depths of the long river that stretched away towards the horizon. Wumbulgal's friends and relations were too frightened to explore the river but Wumbulgal spent many happy days enjoying the beautiful cool water and finding choice things to eat.

One day when the sun was especially hot and the water felt especially and deliciously cool, Wumbulgal went further down the river than she had ever been before. On the bank there were some of the freshest and greenest shoots she had ever seen. Greedily, Wumbulgal waddled up the bank to take a large mouthful. Just as she bit into them she was seized from behind by strong arms. Wumbulgal struggled.

The arms held her tighter and tighter. Wumbulgal called for help but there was no-one to hear her. Still the arms held her and Wumbulgal was dragged into a dark burrow at the water's edge. Poor Wumbulgal, she was sure that her greed had led her into the hands of the water devil who would be sure to kill her.

Inside the burrow it was gloomy dark, but there was enough light for Wumbulgal to see that her captor was not the water devil but only Water Rat. Wumbulgal was so relieved.

'Please let me go,' she quacked. 'I promise I'll go straight back home and leave your green shoots alone.'

'No, little duck,' said Water Rat, 'I shall never let you go. You are the most beautiful little duck I have ever seen and I want you for my wife.'

Wumbulgal was horrified. 'Be your wife?' she said. 'But I am a duck and you are a water rat.

Besides, I am too young to get married. Can you wait until next year?' Wumbulgal thought she would swim home and never come back again.

'No, I can't wait,' said Water Rat. 'I am Goomai, the King of the water rats. It is fitting that I should have a wife as special as you. You must stay with me or I will kill you with my spear.'

Poor Wumbulgal. She had no weapons to use against Water Rat. She had to stay. But all the time she thought about escaping. Her plan was a cunning one. She pretended she was happy with Goomai. She made no attempt to escape from the dark burrow even when she heard her friends and relatives searching the river and calling out for her.

'I like it here with you,' she lied to Goomai.

Soon Goomai believed her. He relaxed his guard and returned to his old habit of sleeping

in the day time and exploring the river at night. Still Wumbulgal bided her time. She stayed by Goomai's side all day, every day, until she was sure that the time was right.

One afternoon when Goomai was in the deepest sleep, Wumbulgal crept out. Without a splash she slipped into the water and paddled her fastest all the way back to her home.

The other ducks were amazed and delighted to see her. They had been sure that the water devil had killed her. Wumbulgal told the whole story and, from then on, neither she nor any other duck ever swam down the river again.

Nesting time came soon after Wumbulgal's return and she, along with all the others, made a cosy nest in the reeds lined with grasses and feathers to keep the eggs warm. At last the eggs hatched. Out came Wumbulgal's tiny babies and proudly she took them down to the water for their first swim.

'What have we here?' asked one of Wumbulgal's snooty relations. 'Your children are most peculiar.'

Wumbulgal was angry. Her children were beautiful. Of course, she could see that they were different from the others. They had four feet instead of two and they had brown fur instead of feathers.

'They look just like Water Rat,' someone else added. 'They are not ducks at all.'

'Take them away, take them away!' shrieked an over-anxious new mother. 'They will grow big and fierce and kill our little darlings.'

Soon all the ducks were quacking furiously. 'Take them away, take them away! They'll kill us, they'll kill us!'

Wumbulgal gathered her little children together. 'Come,' she said proudly, 'we will not stay where we are not wanted.'

Swiftly she led them away upstream, right into the mountains where there were no other ducks to jeer at them. The little ones were quite happy in their new home in the billabong, but Wumbulgal missed the company of her friends and relations and soon she died from sheer loneliness.

And so it was that the first duck-billed platypus came to live in the mountains. They, in turn, laid their eggs and hatched out children until a whole new tribe of animals emerged in the land. Even today, they still live apart from other animals, for no duck ever has four legs and no water rat has ever laid an egg. Wumbulgal, the bold duck who died of loneliness, gave the world a new animal to treasure – the duck-billed platypus.

traditional story retold by Julia Eccleshare

Four little foxes

Speak gently, Spring, and make no sudden sound;
For in my windy valley yesterday I found
New-born foxes squirming on the ground –
    Speak gently.

Walk softly, March, forbear the bitter blow;
Her feet within a trap, her blood upon the snow,
The four little foxes saw their mother go –
    Walk softly.

Go lightly, Spring, Oh, give them no alarm;
When I covered them with boughs to shelter them from harm,
The thin blue foxes suckled at my arm –
    Go lightly.

Step softly, March, with your rampant hurricane;
Nuzzling one another, and whimpering with pain,
The new little foxes are shivering in the rain –
    Step softly.

Lew Sarett

New baby

So there she was, my dark-eyed new sister,
Only a few hours old, sleeping by mother,
I bent over her cot and most gently kissed her,
Feeling so glad that I was her brother.

She looked very tiny, her face rather wrinkled,
With mother soft-smiling that we were together,
Her hair black and shining, her baby hands crinkled,
Born early that evening in cold winter weather.

I gave the glad news to my dog and my tabby cat,
Then went to bed to a night of light dreaming,
Of Ugandan elephants, tigers in Gujerat,
And the sun on their rivers for ever bright gleaming.

But most of my sister, with the sandalwood smelling
Sweetening the air of our small English dwelling.

Leonard Clark

The first day

The spotted fawn
awoke to small leaf-netted suns
tattooing him with coins where he lay
beside his mother's warmth the first day
that gave him light,
the day that played him tunes
in water-music twinkling over stones
and leaf-edged undertones,
the day he learned the feel
of dew on grass
cool, cool, and wet,
of suns that steal the dew with sudden heat,
and heard the fret
in wind-turned willow leaves and wrinkled pool,
the day that filled his lungs with pollened wind
and smell of bracken, earth, and dell-deep moss,
the day he came to know
sharp hunger and the flow
of milk to comfort his small emptiness,
the strangeness of his legs,
the bulwark of his mother's side,
the solace of her pink tongue's first caress,
her snow-soft belly for his sheltering,
the rhythm of his needs
for movement and for rest,
for food and warmth and nest
of flattened grass to fold himself in sleep.

Phoebe Hesketh

Eurynome and the universal egg

In the beginning, there was Eurynome, whose name means 'wide-wandering'. She was the goddess of all things. She came from Chaos, which can be described as an active, barely controllable force. As Eurynome rose up from Chaos, she found nothing solid for her feet to rest upon.

Therefore she divided the sea from the sky, so that there was water and air out of Chaos. She danced, lonely, upon the waves of the sea, and she noticed that her dancing set up a wind behind her. She thought that she would try to create something with this wind, so she wheeled about in her dancing and caught hold of it. She rubbed the wind between her hands, and created the great serpent Ophion.

Then Eurynome took the form of a dove, a sweet, peaceful bird, and brooded upon the water. After some time, she laid the Universal Egg. She directed Ophion to coil his serpent body seven times round this egg, until it hatched, and split in two.

From the egg tumbled out all the things that exist. All the people of the earth tumbled out, of all races and colours. Out tumbled the sun and the moon, so there was light, and the planets and the stars.

The earth tumbled out, with its mountains, plains, hills, rivers and caves. Trees and grasses, plants and flowers tumbled from the egg, and all food-bearing plants.

All living creatures tumbled from the Universal Egg.

Retold by Maureen Stewart

The swallows' creation

Everything was under water.
The trees were wilting,
The flowers had sunk down into
The mud.
There was no grass.
There were no more people.

A hundred years ago there was a flood and the
    world was drowned.
The water rippled in the stars.
Suddenly hundreds of swallows flew
From the east and they were carrying
An enormous sieve made out of china.
They picked up the earth and all the water
Drained out and turned into clouds.

The rowan tree is growing,
The leaves are light green.
Red berries. Red berries.
The green grass is like lots of curved
Eyelashes.
It is a very light night but all
The swallows beating wings down
To the rowan trees make it dark.

When they land they are collecting twigs.
The wings go shhhhoooo.
Some of the swallows are dipping
Into mud puddles.
Everyone is helping to make nests.
One swallow lays three eggs.

One egg cracks then opens
A chick!
One egg cracks and then opens
A girl!
One egg cracks and then opens
A boy!
Slowly the boy and girl climb down
From the nest.
The swallow tells them how
The earth became dry.

That winter the swallow that was
A chick when they were born flies off.
As it leaves them for ever it does
A wing dance.
Shhhhoooo shhhhoooo.

Tansy Hutchinson, aged 8

NEW BEGINNINGS

Spring is the season when many baby animals are born, when plants start growing, the days start to brighten and the whole world seems to be remade. It is a time for thinking about the miracle of life and creation, whatever our religion or beliefs; a time for looking forward and making our own new beginning and for thinking about the future; and a time for considering how we might make the world a better place.

THE TRIMURTI

Hindus have many different stories about the creation of the world. They believe that the world has been made and destroyed many times before and that this will happen again and again.

The Hindus believe in one 'Supreme Spirit', Brahman. The gods Brahma, Vishnu and Shiva are all different forms of Brahman and are known as the 'Trimurti'.

Brahma is believed to be the creator of life, Vishnu the preserver of life, and Shiva the destroyer.

As the creator, it is Brahma who makes the world. Everything from the largest animal to the smallest insect comes from Brahma's body. When Brahma has finished making the world, he then goes to sleep and it is Vishnu who looks after the world.

A day for Brahma lasts more than four thousand million years. When Brahma is sleeping the world grows old and is destroyed by Shiva.

In the morning Brahma awakes and makes the world again.

Jon Mayled

The human life cycle

1. The class can compare newborn babies with children of their own age – physical development, co-ordination, communication, feeding, sleeping and so on. Perhaps mothers with babies and toddlers of different ages could bring them into the classroom and answer questions. The National Childbirth Trust has an education section and may well be able to help arrange for a local volunteer mother to come in. Contact them at Alexandra House, Oldham Terrace, London W3 6NW, tel: 081-992 8637.

2. Make a display of pictures – from magazines, catalogues or the children's own family photographs – showing the stages of physical development from baby to old age. The children·can talk about their perceptions of what life is like at each stage. They could also interview people of different ages, or prepare questionnaires focussing specifically on issues to do with age.

3. Each child could prepare a time line of their own lives from birth to the present day, with photographs, anecdotes and significant dates.

The growth of ideas

Older children could look at the concept of the birth and development of a new idea or ideal which makes a major change in the way people live. They might, for example, study a particular religion – how it started, it's embryonic stage, growth, and development into what we know now. Or they might find out about the growth of an idealistic movement, for example:

- Civil rights – Gandhi, Martin Luther King, Nelson Mandela . . .
- Anti-slavery – Harriet Tubman, Toussaint L'Ouverture, Wilberforce . . .
- Amnesty International
- League of Nations and the United Nations
- The suffragettes

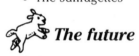

The future

1. Children could prepare another time line which takes them from the present to old age. What are their aspirations for the future? This will also mean thinking about how they think society, technology and the world in general is likely to change.

2. What changes would the children like to see in the world? How might they be brought about? What helpful changes can they, and other people, make in their day-to-day lives? Perhaps together you could prepare a class list of 'spring resolutions'.

New life beginning

New life beginning, come celebrate the birth,
Everybody sing, sing a welcome to the spring.
The season is bringing new hope from Mother Earth,
Everybody welcomes the springtime.

The earth is warming and stirring in the sun,
Everybody sing, sing a welcome to the spring.
The martin, the swift and the swallow will return,
Everybody welcomes the springtime.

Buds on the twig on the branch upon the bough,
Everybody sing, sing a welcome to the spring.
Trees dress in green as the leaves unfold and grow,
Everybody welcomes the springtime.

Lambs in the meadow where once the fields were bare,
Everybody sing, sing a welcome to the spring.
A white butterfly dries her wings upon the air,
Everybody welcomes the springtime.

Words and music by Sandra Kerr

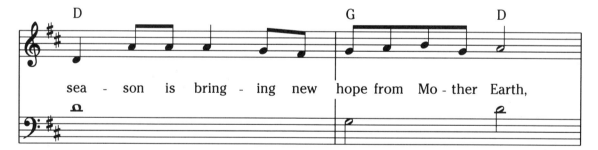

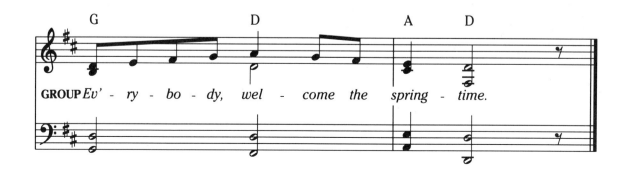

Spring weather

April

So here we are in April, in showy, blowy April,
  In frowsy, blowsy April, the rowdy, dowdy time;
In soppy, sloppy April, in wheezy, breezy April,
  In ringing, stinging April, with a singing swinging rhyme!

The smiling sun of April on the violets is focal,
  The sudden showers of April seek the dandelions out;
The tender airs of April make the local yokel vocal,
  And he raises rustic ditties with a most melodious shout.

So here we are in April, in tipsy gypsy April,
  In flowery, showery April, the twinkly, sprinkly days;
In tingly, jingly April, in highly wily April,
  In mighty, flighty April with its highty-tighty ways!

The duck is fond of April, and the clucking chickabiddy
  And other barnyard creatures have a try at carolling;
There's something in the air to turn a stiddy kiddy giddy,
  And even I am forced to raise my croaking voice and sing.

Ted Robinson

May

There is but one May in the year,
And sometimes May is wet and cold;
There is but one May in the year
Before the year grows old.

Yet though it be the chilliest May,
With least of sun and most of showers,
Its wind and dew, its night and day,
Bring up the flowers.

Christina Rossetti

Spring sayings

When the oak's before the ash,
Then you'll only get a splash.
When the ash is before the oak,
Then you may expect a soak.

A windy March and a rainy April
Make a beautiful May.

March winds and April showers
Bring forth May flowers.

Fog in March, frost in May.

Cast ne'er a clout till may is out.

March comes in like a lion and goes out like a lamb.

April weather, rain and sunshine both together.

In April flood carries away a frog and her brood.

If the wind is in the east on Candlemas Day
There it will stick till the second of May.

When the days begin to lengthen the cold begins to strengthen.

 ## *Keeping weather records*

1. Your class could test the accuracy of some of the spring sayings by keeping a weather diary over several months. (Volunteers will be needed over the Easter holiday.) They could record daily temperatures, hours of daylight, amount and type of cloud, how windy it is and what direction the wind blows from.

2. Some equipment can be made in the classroom. For example, a simple weather vane can be constructed from cardboard, a pin, a length of cane and a compass. Draw an arrow about 8cm long and 1cm wide on the card and cut it out. Carefully push a pin through the arrow and into the cane. To help the arrow turn freely, wiggle the pin from side to side a little to enlarge the hole, then push the two sides gently towards the middle between thumb and forefinger.

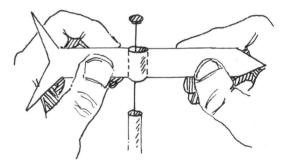

3. Take the weather vane outside and use a compass to find out in which direction the wind turns the arrow. It will point into the wind, so if there is a north wind, the arrow will point north.

4. A group of children could design and construct a more permanent weather vane which could be left outside.

 # RAINBOWS

White light is made up of seven main colours. When light from the sun meets rain it is bent (refracted) as it enters a water droplet, reflected from the back of it, then bent again as it leaves the droplet. The colours bend at slightly different angles so, in effect, the light is split up. We need to stand with our back to the sun in order to see the reflection. The lower the sun in the sky, the bigger the rainbow.

A pilot flying into a rainstorm with the sun behind the plane would see a complete circle.

Rainbows do not usually last for long, but in August 1979 one was recorded in Wales as lasting three hours.

 # RAINBOWS IN MYTHOLOGY

Rainbows are part of the mythology of peoples all over the world, sometimes as good omens, sometimes bad. Celtic lore has it that a crock of gold is buried at the end of each rainbow; all you have to do is find it and dig it up to be rich beyond your wildest dreams.

The Norse myth was that the rainbow was Bifrost's bridge that stretched across the heavens to the kingdom of the gods. The Vikings believed that at the time of Ragnarok the giants in their fiery chariots would ride across the rainbow bridge destroying everything they passed.

Some American Indians believed that the rainbow was a giant bird stranded in the sky world. The coloured bow is the bird's legs and its talons often seized hold of the earth in an attempt to pull itself back down.

In the Bible, after the great flood, God sent a rainbow as a sign of mercy to Noah. It was sent to reassure him that God would never inflict such a disaster again upon the human race.

Australian aborigines believed that the rainbow was the rain's son, protecting his father from falling. They believed that they had to chase the rainbow away in order to prevent drought.

Iris was the Greek goddess of the rainbow who acted as the messenger of the gods.

The Karens of Burma and the Zulus both feared the rainbow, the Karens because they thought it was an evil demon who tried to eat their children and the Zulus because it reminded them of snakes.

 ## *Making rainbows*

1. Children can demonstrate the rainbow effect for themselves. The simplest way is with a glass prism on a sheet of white card. The sunlight is refracted as it passes through, and the seven colours can be seen clearly. You could show them the same effect with a collection of glass objects with sharp angles, such as a mirror with a bevelled edge, a decanter stopper, a cut-glass drinking glass or a crystal ornament.

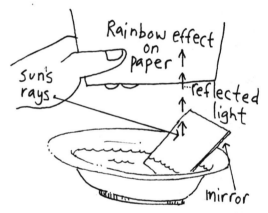

2. On a sunny day, provide children with a bowl of water, a mirror and a sheet of white paper and encourage them to find a way to produce the seven colours. Ask them to explain what happens.

The rainbow

'Make me a bow!'
said Indra
(God of Thunder, Lightning, Rain).
His carpenter raised his head.
'Make me a bow!'
Indra said –
the largest in the land
and my bow must be
the only one of its kind
in the whole Universe.

The carpenter hastened to obey
his mighty Master
and soon he made, of precious wood,
the largest bow that had ever been seen
in the whole Universe.

'Now paint my bow!'
said Indra
(God of Thunder, Lightning, Rain).
His artist – Visvakarma –
raised his head.
'Now paint my bow!'
Indra said –
In colours never known before
in the kingdom of the Gods.

So Visvakarma travelled down
from the Himalaya mountains in the north
to the deep green valleys of the south
to search for new colours
and when he found them
he began to paint the bow
in stripes.

For the first stripe he chose
Violet
the colour of the shimmery mist
at the top of the Himalaya mountains
at dawn.

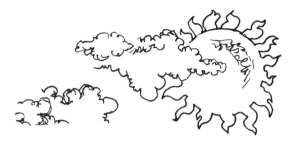

The second stripe he painted
Indigo
the beautiful purpley-blue
that weavers coax out of the indigo plant
to dye their sun-bleached cloths.

For the third stripe he chose
Blue
the glistening blue
of the proud peacock's neck
as he dances in the rain.

The fourth stripe he painted
Green
the raw green of a young mango
before it turns ripe.

For the fifth he chose
Yellow
like the soft downy-fur
of a new-born lion cub.

The sixth stripe he painted
Orange
the colour of the dawn
like the stain of the mehndi plant
that decorates the hands and feet
of girls at festival time.

The seventh stripe was
Red
like the flaming ashoka flowers
in full bloom.

When Visvakarma had finished
he hung the bow out in the sky to dry
but the sun was too hot.
The bow began to bend and crack.
'God Indra!'
begged Visvakarma,
'It is too hot.
Let it rain a little, please.'

Indra looked at the bow of many colours
hanging in the sky
and he was pleased
so he –
'Let it rain a little.'

Visvakarma saw the colours
glowing through the rain
and he was happy.
'Do this every time you use your bow –
God Indra –
Hang it out when the sun is shining
through a little rain.
Then the wood will not crack
and the colours will remain fresh
forever.'

The God of Thunder, Lightning, Rain
took up his mighty bow
and smiled.
And since that day,
each time he uses
his bow of many colours,
he hangs it up in the sky
and children everywhere look up
and laugh
and shout –
'A Rainbow!'

creation myth from India
retold by Beulah Candappa

The last slice of rainbow

Jason walked home from school every day along the side of a steep grassy valley, where harebells grew and sheep nibbled. As he walked, he always whistled. Jason could whistle more tunes than anybody else at school, and he could remember every tune that he had ever heard. That was because he had been born in a windmill, just at the moment when the wind changed from south to west. He could see the wind as it blew; and that is a thing not many people can do. He could see patterns in the stars, too, and hear the sea muttering charms as it crept up the beach.

One day, as Jason walked home along the grassy path, he heard the west wind wailing and sighing. 'Oh woe, woe! Oh, bother and blow! I've forgotten how it goes!'

'What have you forgotten, Wind?' asked Jason, turning to look at the wind. It was all brown and blue and wavery, with splashes of gold.

'My tune! I've forgotten my favourite tune! Oh, woe and blow!'

'The one that goes like this?' said Jason, and he whistled.

The wind was delighted. 'That's it! That's the one! Clever Jason!' And it flipped about him, teasing but kindly, turning up his collar, ruffling his hair. 'I'll give you a present,' it sang, to the tune Jason had whistled. 'What shall it be? A golden lock and a silver key?'

Jason couldn't think what use in the world those things would be, so he said quickly, 'Oh, please, I'd like a rainbow of my very own to keep.'

For, in the grassy valley, there were often beautiful rainbows to be seen, but they never lasted long enough for Jason.

'A rainbow of your own? That's a hard one,' said the wind. 'A very hard one. You must take a pail and walk up over the moor until you come to Peacock Force. Catch a whole pailful of spray from the waterfall. That will take you a long time. But when you have the pail full to the brim, you may find somebody in it who might be willing to give you a rainbow.'

Luckily the next day was Saturday. Jason took a pail, and his lunch, and walked over the moor till he came to the waterfall that was called Peacock Force, because the water, as it dashed over the cliff, made a cloud of spray in which wonderful peacock colours shone and glimmered.

All day Jason stood by the fall, getting soaked, catching the spray in his pail. At last, just at sunset, he had the whole pail filled, right to the brim. And now, in the pail, he saw something that swam swiftly round and round – something that glimmered in brilliant rainbow colours.

It was a small fish.

'Who are you?' said Jason.

'I am the Genius of the Waterfall. Put me back! You've no right to keep me. Put me back and I'll reward you with a gift.'

'Yes,' said Jason quickly, 'yes, I'll put you back, and please may I have a rainbow of my very own, to keep in my pocket.'

'Humph!' said the Genius. 'I'll give you a rainbow, but whether you'll be able to keep it is another matter. Rainbows are not easy to keep. I'll be surprised if you can even carry it home. However, here you are.'

And the Genius leapt out of Jason's pail, in a high soaring leap, back into its waterfall, and, as it did so, a rainbow poured out of the spray and into Jason's pail, following the course of the fish's leap.

'Oh, how beautiful!' breathed Jason, and he took the rainbow from the pail, holding it in his two hands like a scarf, and gazed at its dazzling colours. Then he rolled it up carefully and put it in his pocket.

He started walking home.

There was a wood on his way, and in a dark place among the trees he heard somebody crying pitifully. He went to see what was the matter, and found a badger in a trap.

'Boy, dear, dear boy,' groaned the badger, 'let me out, let me out, or men will come with dogs and kill me.'

'How can I let you out? I'd be glad to, but the trap needs a key.'

'Push in the end of that rainbow I can see in your pocket, you'll be able to wedge open the trap.'

Sure enough, when Jason pushed the end of the rainbow between the jaws of the trap, they sprang open, and the badger was able to clamber out. He made off at a lumbering trot, before the men and dogs could come. 'Thanks, thanks,' he gasped over his shoulder – then he was gone, down his hole.

Jason rolled up the rainbow and put it back in his pocket; but a large piece had been torn off by the sharp teeth of the trap and it blew away.

On the edge of the wood was a little house where old Mrs Widdows lived. She had a very sour nature. If children's balls bounced into her garden, she baked them in her oven until they turned to coal. Everything she ate was black – burnt toast, black tea, black pudding, black olives. She called to Jason, 'Boy, will you give me a piece of that rainbow I see sticking out of your pocket? I'm very ill. The doctor says I need a rainbow pudding to make me better.'

Jason didn't much want to give Mrs Widdows a piece of his rainbow; but she did look ill and poorly, so, rather slowly, he walked into her kitchen, where she cut off a large bit of the rainbow with a breadknife. Then she made a stiff batter, with hot milk and flour and a pinch of salt, stirred in the piece of rainbow, and cooked the mixture. She let it get cold and cut it into slices and ate them with butter and sugar. Jason had a small slice too. It was delicious.

'That's the best thing I've eaten for a year,' said Mrs Widdows. 'I'm tired of black bread and black coffee and black grapes. I can feel this pudding doing me good.'

She did look better. Her cheeks were pink and she almost smiled. As for Jason, after he had eaten his small slice of pudding, he grew eight centimetres.

'You'd better not have any more,' said Mrs Widdows.

Jason put the last piece of rainbow back in his pocket.

There wasn't a lot left now.

As he drew near the windmill where he lived, his sister Tilly ran out to meet him. She tripped over a rock and fell, gashing her leg. Blood poured out of it, and Tilly, who was only four, began to wail. 'Oh, oh, my leg, my leg, my leg! It hurts dreadfully. Oh Jason, please bandage it, please!'

Well, what could he do? Jason pulled the rest of the rainbow from his pocket and wrapped it round Tilly's leg. There was just enough. He tore off a tiny scrap which he kept in his hand.

Tilly was in rapture with the rainbow round her leg. 'Oh! How beautiful! And it has quite stopped the bleeding!' She danced away to show everybody her wonderful rainbow-coloured leg.

Jason was left looking rather sadly at the tiny shred of rainbow beween his thumb and finger. He heard a whisper in his ear, and turned to see the west wind frolicking about the hillside, all yellow and brown and rose-coloured.

'Well?' said the west wind. 'The Genius of the Waterfall did warn you that rainbows are hard to keep! And even without a rainbow, you are a very lucky boy. You can see the pattern of the stars, and hear my song, and you have grown eight centimetres in one day.'

'That's true,' said Jason.

'Hold out your hand,' said the wind.

Jason held out his hand, with the piece of rainbow in it, and the wind blew, as you blow on a fire to make it burn bright. As it blew, the piece of rainbow grew and grew, from Jason's palm, until it lifted up, arching into the topmost corner of the sky; not just a single rainbow, but a double one, with a second rainbow underneath *that*, the biggest and most brilliant that Jason had ever beheld. Many birds were so astonished that they stopped flying and fell to the ground, or collided with each other in mid-air.

Then the rainbow melted and was gone.

'Never mind!' said the west wind. 'There will be another rainbow tomorrow; or if not tomorrow, next week.'

'And I *did* have it in my pocket,' said Jason.

Then he went in for his tea.

Joan Aiken

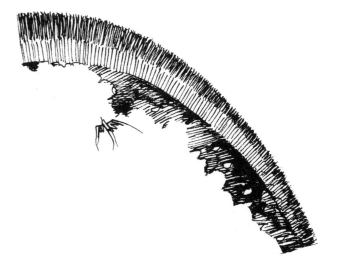

Rainbow

For red, the blood that moves the body.
Red, like a ruby. Red, like a ruby.

For orange, the gentle flame that warms.
Orange, like amber. Orange, like amber.

For yellow, the sun shines on the earth.
Yellow, like topaz. Yellow, like topaz.

For green, the turtle in waters clear.
Green, like emerald. Green, like emerald.

For blue, the blue of mountain light.
Blue, like a sapphire. Blue, like a sapphire.

For indigo, worn with naval pride.
Indigo, so dark. Indigo, so dark.

And violet, walking in fields of flowers.
Violet, amethyst. Violet, amethyst.

Philip John Ellis, aged ten

Spring changes

A – ah, the weather in springtime,
O – oh, the weather in spring.
A – ah, the weather in springtime,
O – oh, the weather in spring.
And you never know, it changes so,
O – oh, the weather in spring!

I wonder whether the weather
  is going to be cold or hot.
Is it going to be windy
  or rainy or sunny or what?
Under the weather in springtime
  you can get quite vexed,
When the sun comes out one minute,
  and its freezing cold the next.
  A – ah the weather in springtime,
  O – oh, the weather in spring.
  A – ah, the weather in springtime,
  O – oh, the weather in spring.
  And you never know, it changes so,
  Oh, you never know, the wind might blow,
  O – oh, the weather in spring.

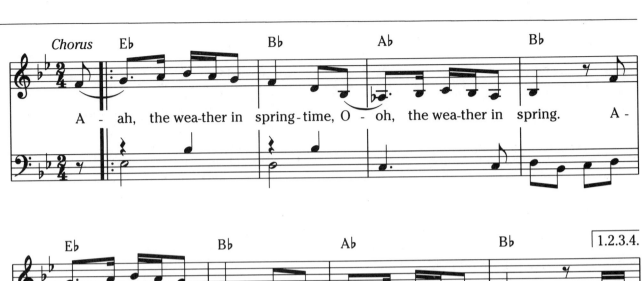

Oh, will I need an umbrella,
  is it going to be dry or wet?
If I leave it at home,
  it's sure to rain, I bet.
The weather in March and April
  can get you really vexed,
When the sun comes out one minute,
  and it pours with rain the next.
  A – ah, the weather in springtime,
  O – oh, the weather in spring.
  A – ah, the weather in springtime,
  O – oh, the weather in spring.
  And you never know, it changes so,
  Oh, you never know, the wind might blow,
  Oh, you never know, you might see a rainbow,
  O – oh, the weather in spring.

I think I'll go to the rainbow's end,
  and find a pot of gold,
So what's the weather today?
  Is it going to be hot or cold?
Oh, the weather in springtime,
  it puts you to the test,
Should I wear another jumper,
  or perhaps leave off my vest!
  A – ah, the weather in springtime,
  O – oh, the weather in spring.
  A – ah, the weather in springtime,
  O – oh, the weather in spring.
  And you never know, it changes so,
  Oh, you never know, the wind might blow,
  Oh, you never know, you might see a rainbow,
  You never know, it just might snow,
  O – oh, the weather in spring.

Words and music by Harriet Powell

The animal world

Coming out of hibernation

Black bats hang in barns,
their wings folded
like old umbrellas.

Snoring hedgehogs sleep
curled up
like hairbrushes
beneath crisp leaves.

Grey squirrels dream
in dreys of scrambled twigs.

Toads squat,
their eyelids drawn down,
as still as stones
tucked beneath
damp earth.

Sly spring sunlight
creeps through clouds,
bulbs break the earth
and the world wears
a new coat.

Bats stretch their creased wings
and blink their way
from hollow tree stumps.

Hedgehogs uncurl
and sniff,
sipping the sunlight.

The blotched toad
gulps in warm air;
he puffs his wrinkled cheeks
like an old man.

The squirrel stretches
her arched back
and tests a branch.
Like a rat she runs
to find her acorn stash.

The world rolls on to its side
and stretches out its legs.
It reaches for its sunglasses
and rubs its earthy hands.
The spring sings out loud.

Pie Corbett

The nest

Don't move –
   don't touch –
don't speak –
   do you see
a blackbird's nest
   in the holly tree?

Look very carefully
   in between
last year's prickle
   and this year's green

Timid and brown
   the mother bird
listens, and watches.
   Has she heard?

Whisper –
   whisper –
do you see
   a blackbird's nest
in the holly tree?

Jean Kenward

BIRDS' NESTS

Birds nest in many different places – in trees and bushes, and sometimes on the ground. Their nests need to provide safety from predators and shelter from the weather. Ground-built nests, such as skylarks', are usually well camouflaged to make them safer.

In Britain, rooks are among the first birds to nest in spring and often start looking for a suitable site as early as January. Their favourite nesting site is an elm tree.

Nests are made from a variety of different materials, depending on where they are sited. Birds such as blackbirds, which nest in trees and hedgerows, use twigs and grass, and line the nest with soft grass held together with mud. Others, such as martins and swallows, use a combination of mud and straw. The South American ovenbird is an expert builder and often constructs a domed nest of mud on fence posts. Kingfishers dig their nests out of stream or river banks, hollowing out a tunnel up to one metre long which leads to a small chamber where the eggs are laid. The weaver bird gets its name from the intricate way it uses its feet and beak to knot together a framework of grass and twigs. In Holland, storks fly in from Africa, and make untidy nests of twigs on chimney stacks. Woodpeckers nest safely in holes in trees, while seabirds are more likely to have open, unprotected nests, laying their eggs in a dip in the ground or on a ledge on a cliff. Cuckoos, of course, don't build nests at all.

Once birds have reared their young, their nests are abandoned, although well-built nests might be adapted and used by another species during the following breeding season.

HIBERNATION

There are many different levels of hibernation. In some mammals, for example, the body temperature falls to only a few degrees above the surrounding air. These include dormice, chipmunks, hedgehogs and bats. Others, such as bears and squirrels, don't lose much body heat and are in a deep sleep rather than true hibernation. Some wake up occasionally for food, others sleep undisturbed for up to six months. All hibernating animals have a slower pulse and breathing rate. The little marmot breathes only once in three minutes. Some animals, such as bats, wake up very quickly, with a fast temperature rise, others take several hours.

Fly away, swallow!

Fly away, fly away, over the sea,
Sun-loving swallow, for summer is done.
Come again, come again, come back to me,
Bringing the summer and bringing the sun.

Christina Rossetti

MIGRATION

Migration has puzzled people for centuries. It was once believed that birds hibernated at the bottom of ponds, or flew away to the moon when they disappeared in autumn. Animals migrate in order to find the right feeding or breeding environment. Through migration they can avoid tough winter conditions by moving to warmer climes where more food is available.

Swallows are among the most familiar migrants. When they fly south for the winter they usually visit the same places year after year, returning north in the spring to the nesting areas in which they were born. Their round trip is several thousand miles long. Swallows migrate for food – during the spring and summer in the northern hemisphere they lay their eggs and rear their young on plentiful insects. When the weather cools and the insects die off, they fly south to find a new supply.

Other animals which migrate include butterflies, whales, turtles and caribou. The latter migrate as far as 800 miles overland to the forests of southern Canada for winter food. Green turtles swim from their breeding areas on Ascension Island in mid-Atlantic to feeding areas off the coast of Brazil. Salmon migrate from the rivers where they spawned to the ocean. They live there for two or three years before returning to the same spawning grounds, where they mate, lay eggs and then die. Humpback whales live in both Arctic and Antarctic waters, but the water there is too cold for their young, so they migrate to warmer water near the equator to breed.

The cuckoo

Cuckoo, Cuckoo,
What do you do?

In April
I open my bill.

In May
I sing night and day.

In June
I change my tune.

In July
Away I fly.

Anon

Plotting migrations

Using reference material, children could research the migration patterns of different creatures. You could limit it to visitors to Britain, chiefly birds, or do a wider study including many other animals. Graphs can be drawn comparing times of year of migration and the lengths of the routes. If you display a large map of the appropriate area of the world, routes can be drawn on using different colours for different animals. If you want to reuse the map, routes could be marked with lengths of wool (although many migration routes are not straight). Alternatively, you could put a sheet of clear plastic over the map and mark the routes on that. A group of children could even prepare a presentation using overlaying foils on an overhead projector.

 ## METAMORPHOSIS

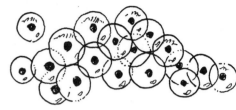

In March frogs begin to breed, usually returning to the ponds where they were born. Inside the frog spawn tiny tadpoles can be seen as black dots. Toad spawn is similar to frog spawn, but is laid in long strings, rather than clusters.

The spawn turns into frogs within about four weeks. A week after laying, tadpoles emerge from the jelly. They breathe through gills, and eat plants from the pond. Gradually they lose their gills and develop lungs, and also start eating flies and worms.

The life cycle of a butterfly is longer. The eggs laid by an adult butterfly on leaves hatch into larvae or caterpillars, which eat a great deal and grow very quickly, shedding their skins several times. The larvae then develop hard cases, inside which their bodies re-form. At this stage they are known as pupae, and many insects survive the winter in this form. Eventually, the pupae hatch into butterflies. The first butterfly to emerge in the spring is the brimstone, which is yellow with an orange spot on each wing.

Grasshoppers and crickets develop in a different way. Their eggs hatch into nymphs, immature insects which resemble the adults but which do not have wings or reproductive organs. The nymphs are covered in a hard shell or skin, known as the cuticle. Every now and then the shell splits open, to reveal a new soft shell underneath. Each time a nymph moults its shell, its wings grow a little more until they are finally ready to fly.

black dot

a black dot   a scum-nail   a cool kicker   a panting puffer   a high hopper   a catalogue
a jelly tot   a jiggle-tail   a sitting slicker   a fly-snuffer   a belly-flopper   to make me

Libby Houston   frog

Keep a frog log

Keeping a frog log can help a child observe the life cycle of a creature and the process of metamorphosis.

Frog spawn should be collected in enough pond water to enable the frog spawn to float in a deep container. A fish tank or a large washing-up bowl can be used. As the container must have a large surface area to provide sufficient oxygen absorption, jam-jars, goldfish bowls and buckets are not suitable. Some pond weed should be placed in the tank along with some large stones in the centre. These will enable the baby frogs to climb out of the water to breathe air.

When the tadpoles hatch from the spawn they will eat plant food from the weed and tiny plants from the water. When the 'leg buds' appear, the tadpoles should be fed with small pieces of fresh raw meat. Any meat that is not eaten must be removed from the tank before it contaminates the water.

Once the metamorphosis has been completed *the baby frogs should be returned to the pond* where the spawn was collected.

A log can be made charting all the stages of development. If the spawn is divided when first collected, one lot could be kept in the classroom and the other outside in a safe place. The rates of development can then be compared.

In classroom	Date Collected	Eggs hatched	Gills disappeared	Hind legs appeared	Front legs appeared	Tail disappeared
First	28 Mar	3 April	10 April			
Last	28 Mar	5 April				
Outside						
First	28 Mar	3 April	10 April			
Last	28 March	6 April				

Miracle

In June after a brief shower
an astounding appearance of little green frogs
as if a miracle had happened,
and they had fallen down from heaven.

In March they choked the pools and ditches,
and then masses of black-centred jelly eggs
floating with moorhens and tiny water-boatmen,
speckled trout rising.

April, legions of darting tadpoles,
needle tails and bullet heads growing,
until, one evening, the cycle almost over,
first frogs leaping out
to cover the land like a plague.

The frenzied croaking died down,
they move solitary into damp garden corners,
under stones, on to reedy river banks,
juicy prey for sharp-eyed heron.

Next year, the same miracle.

Leonard Clark

Butterfly

Butterfly on the wall –
    butterfly, with your blue
and decorated wings –
    How do you do?

April is in the air,
    the frost is gone.
What was it made you put
    your colours on?

All winter long your wings
    were folded close
in a dark, secret place . . .
    Nobody knows

How the sun touched you with
    his finger, then
told you the spring had come.
    O when, O when

You felt his burning gold
    what did you do?
Did you fly after him –
    blue into blue?

Jean Kenward

Observing a caterpillar

A caterpillar can be kept for a short time in the classroom for children to observe. Warn them not to touch any caterpillar with hairs as they can cause a rash. Caterpillars should not be picked up with the fingers in case they get squashed. The best way is to pick the piece of the plant the caterpillar is on (with permission of the owner) and transfer it to a container.

Encourage the children to look at the caterpillar very closely. They could use a magnifying glass or put the caterpillar in a magnispector – a special container big enough to keep the creature and some of its plant food in, and which has a magnifying lid.

A caterpillar has been described as an eating machine. *Don't keep it away from its food supply for too long*, and put it back where it was found as soon as possible, unless you can keep it properly.

How many legs has the caterpillar got? How are they spaced out on the body?
Are they all the same? Are they all used in the same way?
How many segments does its body have? Do all caterpillars have the same number?
How does it eat? Which way do its jaws move? Does it eat a hole in a leaf or chew all round the edge?

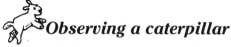
Studying the life cycles of butterflies and moths

If you want children to study live creatures at first hand you will need to make sure you can provide the right conditions in the classroom to rear them. One book with good advice is *A complete guide to British butterflies* by Margaret Brooks and Charles Knight, published by Cape. The *Butterflies and moths* and *Caterpillars* cards from the Harcourt, Brace, Jovanovich 'Minibeasts' series are excellent for children wanting to make detailed studies.

Lavinia Bat

Hanging head down in her winter sleep Lavinia Bat was quite comfortable. Her winter dreams were always pleasant, always slow, never hurried.

In her dream the night was a lantern-globe of sound, it was lit with the colour of the wind, the rolling of the earth, the starfires of crickets. It made a gentle hissing as it turned in space and all the skies turned with it.

Lavinia woke up, still half in her dream. She washed herself and stretched her wings and did her waking-up exercises. She flew up and down her cave, she did loops and turns, she did rolls and dives and figure eights. Then she went back to sleep.

In her dreams Lavinia heard a whispering, she listened to it carefully.

'Pass it on,' said the whispering.

'Pass what on?' said Lavinia.

'The something from the other,' said the whispering.

'What other?' said Lavinia.

'The other dream,' said the whispering.

Nights and days passed, the moon grew fat, grew thin, grew fat, grew thin. The skunk cabbages pushed up green points out of the ground, then the Jack-in-the-pulpits stood up in the boggy places and Big John Turtle climbed on to a log and tried out the sunlight.

Lavinia woke up. All she could remember was, 'Pass it on'. But she couldn't remember what the something was that she was meant to pass on.

It was evening, it was spring, it was time to get moving. Outside the cave everything smelled wet and muddy and new.

What a singing there was at the pond! Jugs-of-rum were sung by the bullfrogs, while others claimed that the water was only knee-deep, knee-deep. The peepers peeped constantly but they never told what they saw. 'We peep, we peep!' was all they would say. Some of the insects said that Katy did, some said that Katy didn't, no one knew for sure.

Lavinia put her FM echolocator on SCAN, she put her computer on AUTOMATIC and she was ready to go. Other bats were coming out as well, all frequency bands were clicking and buzzing as they scrambled skitter-scattering, cornering into the night, they hadn't eaten since autumn.

What a skirmish for supper! The darkness was full of buzzing, whirring, and flapping things to eat.

CLICK CLICK CLICK CLICK CLICK, went Lavinia's scanner as it made its sweep, 'BZZZZZZZZZZZ!' as she zeroed in on her prey. Fat moths looped and turned and rolled and dived and Lavinia looped and turned and rolled and dived with them, some she caught and some she missed.

'JUG-OF-RUM!' sang Jim Frog and his crowd.

'Knee-deep!' sang the others.

'We peep!' sang the peepers.

'Katy did!' sang the katydids.

'Katy didn't!' sang the katydidnt's.

'WHOOHOOHOO!' hooted Ephraim Owl.

'BLEAK OUTLO news and weather!' whispered Charlie Meadows.

'MOTH AT SIX O'CLOCK!' said Lavinia's scanner. 'FOUR METRES AND CLOSING, THREE METRES, TWO . . .'

'DIVE!' said Lavinia's computer.

'I TASTE AWFUL!' ultrasounded the moth.

'Ptui!' said Lavinia, zooming out of her dive and zeroing in on another moth.

'I TASTE AWFUL TOO!' ultrasounded that one.

'No, you don't,' said Lavinia. SCHLOOP! What a supper that was, the first night of the spring outcoming!

Lavinia was listening to the night all round her and she was listening inside herself as well. She was going to have a baby.

'Ah!' said Lavinia, clicking to herself. She half-remembered something but she half-forgot it at the same time.

When Lavinia's time came her baby was born, it was a daughter and Lavinia named her Lola.

Lola was clever, she wanted to know about everything. She said to Lavinia, 'How do you do bat work?'

Lavinia said, 'Hang on and I'll show you.'

Lola hung on and Lavinia showed her.

'The main thing,' said Lavinia, 'is to get tuned in.'

'Tuned in to what?' said Lola.

'Everything,' said Lavinia. She took Lola hunting with her and Lola got tuned in. She got tuned in to the night, she got tuned in to moving with it. Soon Lola was ready to hunt for herself. Off she went, cornering in to the night.

Lavinia remembered her dreams then, remembered the lantern-globe of night, the hissing of it as it turned in space. Lavinia remembered the whispering that had said, 'Pass it on!'

'Ah!' said Lavinia, clicking and buzzing, sweeping the night with her scanner and rolling with the rolling world.

'Ah!' said Lavinia, tuned into everything. 'I've done that!'

Russell Hoban

I'm a chick I am

I'm a chick I am,
I'm big and brave and strong,
My feathers are bright and yellow
But my beak's not very long.
When I grow up, I'll grow to be a cock,
Making sure that nobody stays asleep,
    But when it's spring
    And the buds are opening,
    I'll stretch my neck,
    Strut about, shout aloud,
    Cheep, cheep, cheep.

I'm a lamb I am,
I'm big and brave and strong,
My wool is tight and curly,
But it won't grow very long,
When I grow up I'll grow to be a sheep,
I'll crop the grass and wander near and far.
    But when it's spring
    And the buds are opening,
    Watch me jump, twist and turn,
    Frolic and run,
    Baaa, baaa, baaa.

I'm a tadpole I am,
I'm big and brave and strong,
I'm very good at swimming,
But my legs aren't very long,
When I grow up I'll grow to be a frog,
I'll hop and jump and swim just like a fish.
    But when it's spring
    And the buds are opening,
    I'll dart and dive,
    Flick the water with my tale,
    Splash, splosh, splish.

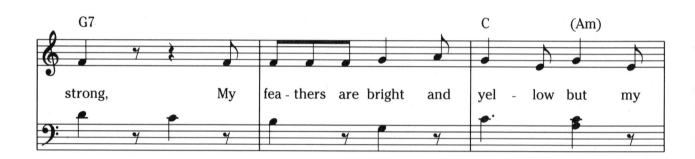

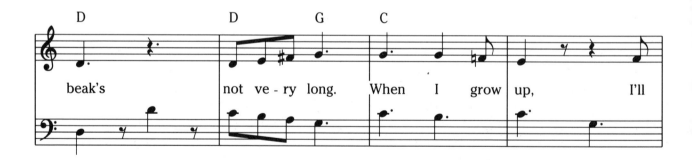

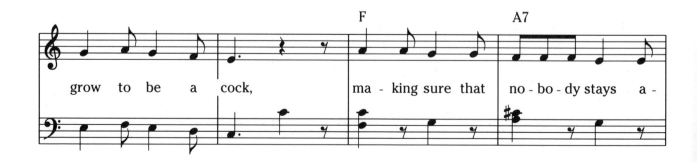

I'm a caterpillar I am,
I'm big and brave and strong,
My body's brown and furry,
But it won't be for very long,
When I grow up, I'll grow to be a moth,
Fluttering over meadow, hill and swamp.
    But now it's spring,
    And the buds are opening,
    I'll climb a stalk,
    Find a nice juicey leaf,
    Chomp, chomp, chomp.

Words and music by David Moses

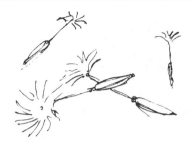

The growing season

Our trees in spring

The silver birch is a dainty lady,
   She wears a satin gown;
The elm tree makes the old churchyard shady,
   She will not live in town.

The English oak is a sturdy fellow,
   He gets his green coat late;
The willow is smart in a suit of yellow,
   While brown the beech trees wait.

Such a gay green gown God gave the larches –
   As green as He is good!
The hazels hold up their arms for arches,
   When Spring rides through the wood.

The chestnut's proud, and the lilac's pretty,
   The poplar's gentle and tall,
But the plane tree's kind to the poor dull city,
   I love him best of all.

E. Nesbitt

I planted some seeds

I planted some seeds
In my garden today.
They haven't come up yet,
I hope they're okay.

Should I dig them all up,
Take them back to the shop?
Ask for my money back,
Say they're a flop?

Perhaps they are faulty,
Perhaps they were duff,
Maybe they haven't
Been watered enough.

I planted some seeds
In my garden today.
They haven't come up yet,
I hope they're okay.

Colin McNaughton

Climbing to heaven

It was early spring and soon it would be time for the rice to be planted. One by one the villagers began to prepare their fields. First the hard clumps of earth had to be broken up and the fields smoothed and ploughed. At last, only Yasohachi's field stood out, lumpy and uneven. While the other villagers worked and struggled with the earth *he* put up a notice in the village.

'What game do you think you're playing, Yasohachi?' said his master.

'Your field is still as lumpy as the back of a toad and yet you waste your time putting up this ridiculous notice: 'On Sunday at four o'clock Yasohachi will climb from his field to heaven.'

But Yasohachi just smiled. 'I haven't got time to explain, master. I'm off to make the climb right now.'

Yasohachi marched off to his field and his master followed on behind, finding it hard to keep up with his pace.

A large crowd of villagers had already gathered in the field. They were milling about, peering at a long pole standing upright in the ground. They found it hard to keep steady on their feet – one foot would be up on a great lump of earth, while the other foot was down in a hole. Yasohachi pushed his way through and grasping the pole firmly with one hand he spoke to the crowd:

'Ladies and gentlemen. Watch closely. And forget nothing when you proudly tell your children and grandchildren that *you* were present on the famous Sunday when, at four o'clock, Yasohachi climbed from his field to heaven.'

He took hold of the pole with both hands and pulled himself up. He paused for a moment, reached up with his hands, and pulled again. A gasp went through the crowd as the pole began to lean. The next moment the villagers had scattered in all directions, running, stumbling and tripping over the uneven earth.

Most of them had already fallen to the ground as Yasohachi landed with a crash. But he was up quicker than any of them. While they were still dusting themselves down, he had walked off a few paces and replanted the pole firmly in the earth. Up he went again – one pull, two pulls – he was over half way. But on the third pull the pole swayed, the crowd scattered, and down came Yasohachi.

Two hours later, the dusty, earth-spattered villagers were straggling back home.

'Didn't I say he'd never be able to do it?'

'It's not natural.'

'Climbing to heaven on a pole.'

Yasohachi and his master stood in the middle of the field alone.

'I think I'll start planting tomorrow.'

But his master scowled. He scowled at Yasohachi and the now perfectly smooth field stretching out around them.

Japanese story
retold by Eric Hadley and Tessa Hadley

A wondrous thing

Long, long ago, no one knows where and no one knows when, a grey farm cat had a litter of kittens. She hid them in a corner of a dark shed. These were not the first, nor the last kittens to be hidden so. That has always been the way of cats.

The kittens were very like any breed of new kitten that you may have been lucky enough to see. Tiny, frail, sprawling, grey mewlings with tightly closed eyes. They were feeble and they were helpless, and the farmer, not wanting more cats about, hunted until he found them. Four tiny cats! He scooped them up into his hat then strode out of the shed to the river. The Mother Cat followed anxiously, mewing her concern to him. The farmer ignored her cries. He threw the kittens into the river as if they were stones, then went back to his house.

Their mother was frantic. She ran crying along the bank. Scratching! Clawing! Desperately she tried to find a way down the banks which were as steep as walls. She couldn't reach the water and her mews were piteous. Her voice grew high and thin with grief. The birds stopped singing. Bees stopped buzzing. Grasshoppers stopped clicking wings. In their silence it was as if all creatures were listening to the cat's wails for her kittens.

Now, on the far bank of the river grew a row of trees with slim branches which trailed leaves towards the water. And, as if the trees had seen the kittens' plight, their branches drooped lower and lower into the river. Long slender stems and narrow leaves ribboned outwards towards the kittens, to dip and twist under the small struggling bodies, to overlap and weave a floating cradle of leaves.

Kittens' paws grasped at twigs and stems.

Kittens' paws clung tightly to the leaf cradle. It floated them down the stream.

Eagerly the Mother Cat scrambled along the bank, keeping pace with the rescued kittens. She mewed soft encouraging little sounds until the kittens reached the shallows, below the clump of river trees. Here the cliff-bank fell away to a crossing.

A sure-footed leap and the cat crossed to her kittens, then one by one, by the scruff of its neck, she carried each one ashore.

She made a nest for her kittens in the roots of the trees. And it was a well-hidden, low-down, hide-away, secret nest which no one ever found.

The kittens grew into cats and as summer passed into winter, the leaves of the river-bank trees turned from green to gold. Then autumn winds stripped the branches bare for winter's cold.

When spring came the glossy buds swelling on the branches did not burst to unfold new leaves as had happened in other years. Instead, each branch was shyly decked with grey blossoms as sleek as kittens' fur. Never before had the trees flowered.

Each year since, the same flowers have appeared.

No one knows where and no one knows when the trees were first called Pussy Willows but they still grow well in watery places. Should you have the chance, feel the little catkin bud. And that will be a wondrous thing for you.

Jean Chapman

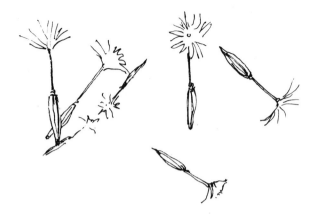

PLANT LORE

In the past, it was common for planting to be timed around the phases of the moon. Some seeds would be planted with the new moon and others immediately after the new moon.

Crops planted at full moon were supposed to ripen earlier than those planted at the wane.

Sow new beans when the moon is round
They'll pod down to the ground.

After a rainy winter a fruitful spring.

March flowers make no summer bowers.

March dry good rye. March wet good wheat.

Cut a thistle in May, he'll be there next day.
Cut a thistle in June, he'll come again soon.
Cut him in July and he's sure to die!

Twelfth of May, Stow Fair Day,
Sow your kidney beans today.

Who weeds in May
Throws all away!

When April blows her horn
It's good for both hay and corn.

The seed

How does it know,
this little seed,
if it is to grow
to a flower or a weed,
if it is to be
a vine or a shoot,
or grow to a tree
with a long deep root?
A seed so small
where do you suppose
it stores up all
of the things it knows?

Aileen Fisher

Seeds

The seeds I sowed –
For weeks unseen –
Have pushed up pygmy
Shoots of green;
So frail you'd think
The tiniest stone
Would never let
A glimpse be shown.
But no; a pebble
Near them lies,
At least a cherry-stone
In size,
Which that mere sprout
Has heaved away,
To bask in sunshine,
See the day.

Walter de la Mare

The catkin

Walking up the branch
Of the long
Pussy willow tree
Go the catkins
To settle in one place
Like cats' paws
Close to the stem
And all of a sudden they flower
Yellow bitty pollen
Blows around
A yellow mist
A dusty spray of soft gentle powder
In a yellow
Puddle.

Lindsay Holley, aged 8

PLANT LIFE CYCLES

The life cycle of a plant starts with a seed. Seeds are well adapted to survive the winter until conditions are right for them to germinate. Inside their hard coats they have a food supply which keeps them alive until spring. In order for a seed to germinate it needs water, oxygen and a temperature above freezing.

Plants have different life cycles depending partly on the climate and environment they live in. Many garden flowers are annuals, growing and flowering during the spring and summer when it is warm. When winter comes, their leaves and flowers die, leaving behind the seeds which will turn into new plants.

Other garden flowers are perennials which can survive the cold of winter. During the cold weather they are dormant, losing their leaves, and living off the food stored in the stem and roots.

Flowers such as the crocus are especially associated with spring. The flower comes from a brown corm or bulb which remains dormant below ground during the winter. As the days begin to grow longer and the temperature rises, the bulb sprouts, and the miniature flower bud and leaves which have been hidden inside appear above ground.

Catkins are another sign of spring; these appear on several different types of trees including the alder, hazel and willow. Elm trees have small, fuzzy flowers with red stamens.

Growing seeds in a jar

You will need:

a clean jar – a jam jar, large plain coffee jar or plastic sweet jar
blotting paper or absorbent kitchen paper
small sticky labels
water
different types of seeds – beans and peas germinate quickly
tracing paper

What to do

1 Line the jam jar with blotting paper or several layers of absorbent kitchen paper.

2 Place the seeds between the paper and the jar. Do not put them too close together. It might be easier if you damp the paper first.

3 Write the name of each seed on a small label and stick it just to the side of each seed, so it won't obscure any growth.

4 Wrap some tracing paper round the jar and secure it.

5 A child can now trace the shape of each seed and write its name.

6 Put a little water in the bottom of the jar to keep the paper damp for several days.

7 Observe what happens to the seeds. After a few days the shoots will start growing upwards and the roots downwards. Ask some children to trace the shape of any growth. Remove the paper, write the date on it and wrap a new piece round the jar.

8 Repeat this procedure every day or so. The different pieces of tracing paper will give the children a very clear record so they can compare the stages of growth of the various seeds.

Other jars of seeds can be grown at the same time, each one grown under different conditions – no water, jar filled with water, no light, no warmth, lid kept on jar and so on.

Try an experiment to see what happens if the seeds are inverted after they have started sprouting and growing. Leave them for a few days and you should see that they have changed direction so that the roots are growing downwards again.

When the growth is well established the seedlings can be potted and grown.

Growing other plants

Avocados, sweet potatoes or hyacinth bulbs can be suspended over a dish of water. Stick four cocktail sticks into the seed near its base. Balance this over the dish so the base of the seed is in the water. Alternatively, use a special bulb holder which can be bought commercially. Crocuses can also be grown without soil. Put some pebbles in a bowl, stand the bulbs on them, then fill in the gaps with more pebbles. Put a little water in the bottom. Keep the dish in a light place, and make sure there is always some water in the bottom. If you use a transparent container, children will be able to see the root growth.

Making a seed stencil

Cress or mustard seed grows very quickly on damp cotton wool or kitchen roll. Interesting shapes, patterns or words can be made by planting the seeds through a stencil which is then removed.

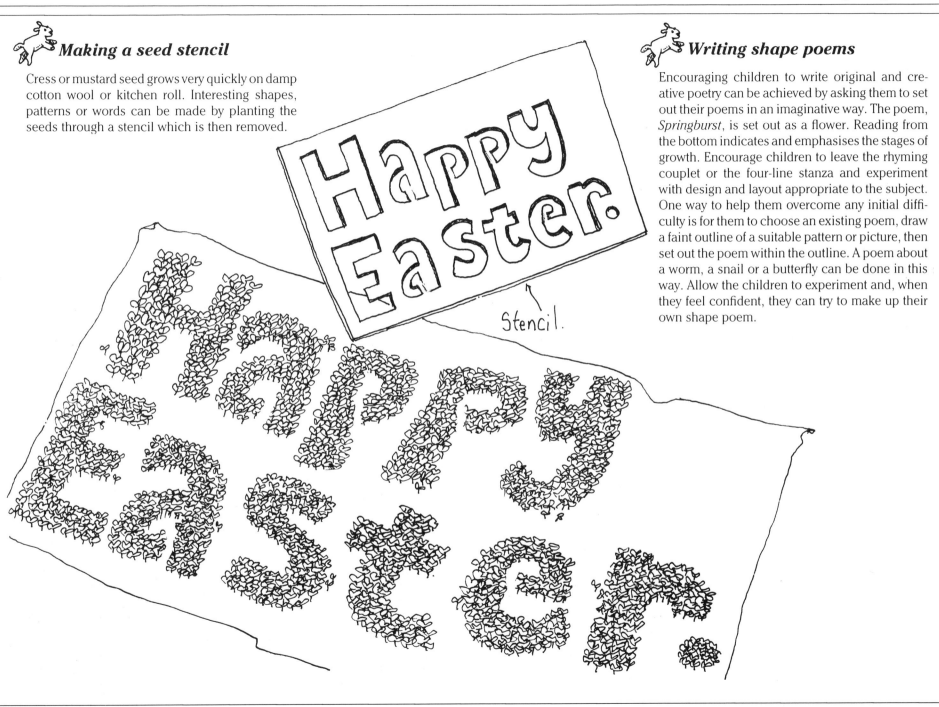

Stencil.

Writing shape poems

Encouraging children to write original and creative poetry can be achieved by asking them to set out their poems in an imaginative way. The poem, *Springburst*, is set out as a flower. Reading from the bottom indicates and emphasises the stages of growth. Encourage children to leave the rhyming couplet or the four-line stanza and experiment with design and layout appropriate to the subject. One way to help them overcome any initial difficulty is for them to choose an existing poem, draw a faint outline of a suitable pattern or picture, then set out the poem within the outline. A poem about a worm, a snail or a butterfly can be done in this way. Allow the children to experiment and, when they feel confident, they can try to make up their own shape poem.

Star flower

Star flower O,
Star flower O,
Star flower in the ground O,
Who would ever know such a flower O,
Would be shining all around O,
Shining all around?

Star flower O,
Star flower O,
Star flower by the reed O,
Who would ever know such a flower O,
Would be hiding in a seed O,
Hiding in a seed?

Words and music by Malvina Reynolds

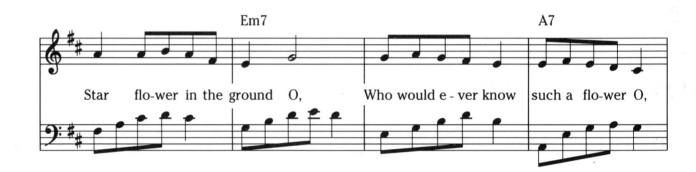

Would be shi-ning all a - round O, Shi-ning all a - round.

Springburst

(to be read from the bottom)

FLOWER!

the

slowly   slowly

the *petal* curling

the *bud*,

awakening.

Oh, the

up!

straight

I know!
Now
hm.
hm
see.   Hm   see.
me Let Let me
higher . . .
must reach

for the sky –
Now, must reach
I be!
I live!

up
tip
warmth
coolness
water,
food and
life growing,
life, being,
in the dark –

(seed style)
spark
A

John Travers Moore

Customs and festivals

In almost every country which has a springtime (unlike the tropics which basically have two seasons, rainy and dry) there are spring festivals and traditional customs. They celebrate the end of the dark days of winter and welcome the season of growth, the renewal of life and the strengthening power of the sun. Fire, often the symbol of the sun, is an important part of many of the traditions. (See, for example, *Holi* and the *Paschal candle*, pages 58 and 66.) There is the practical reason of getting rid of the winter's rubbish, and the symbolic one of the destruction of evil.

Other devices for driving away evil spirits were loud noises and fearsome masks and costumes. Mock battles were fought representing the triumph of spring over winter (see Roger McGough's poem on page 9). Springtime was often a time of mayhem. Apprentice boys in England were usually given the day off on Shrove Tuesday and indulged in wild pranks and fierce football games. These were condemned but still survive in some places in slightly less violent form. At Ashbourne in Derbyshire, for instance, there is a Shrove Tuesday football match which goes on all afternoon and much of the night, and where the goals are three miles apart with

a stream in the middle. A similar event happens in Hallaton, Leicestershire, where the 'ball' is a small beer cask. The Hindu festival of Holi (see page 66) also has the element of mischief and the Sikh festival Hola Mohalla traditionally features three days of sports and physical games.

Other spring festivals are more gentle. The Dutch flower parades, the Japanese Cherry Blossom festival and even the Chelsea Flower Show are all celebrations of the return of growth and colour. St David's Day, with its symbols of the leek for winter and the daffodil for spring derives from a spring festival, as does St Patrick's Day, now celebrated in New York particularly with a grand parade.

For some, it is also New Year, and for many it is a time for making a fresh start. (See *New beginnings*, page 20.) Some Buddhists celebrate their new year, Wesak, some time in April or May, depending on the moon. For those of the Bahai faith 21st March is New Year, Naw Ruz, as it is for Parsis, Jamshedi Naoroze. The Parsis celebrate with present-giving, new clothes, special foods and decorated houses. For many Christians, Easter too is a time for wearing new clothes.

SPRING CLEANING

Cleaning the home after the winter may not be a festival in itself, but it is a firmly entrenched custom in many cultures, and is often linked to a spring festival.

Early spring was thought to be the time for a 'clean sweep'; a time to get rid of the old and remove anything evil from the home. Jewish Passover (see page 72) is preceded by a thorough cleaning of the house and before the Hindu festival of Holi (see page 66) houses are cleaned and all the rubbish accumulated over the winter months is burnt on the Holi bonfires. This act is symbolic of the victory of good over ill, the destruction of winter and the welcoming of spring.

The Japanese festival of Setsubun, the 'change of season', is celebrated by scattering roasted beans around the home and throwing them into the streets at imaginary devils. This served as a reminder to make a new start and rid the home of misfortune, sickness or anything evil.

Although cleaning in spring is usually symbolic of good removing evil from the home, there is one old English superstition which says that a house should not be swept on Good Friday because the life of one of the family would be swept away.

Mole gives up spring cleaning

The Mole had been working very hard all the morning, spring-cleaning his little home. First with brooms, then with dusters; then on ladders and steps and chairs, with a brush and a pail of whitewash; till he had dust in his throat and eyes, and splashes of whitewash all over his black fur, and an aching back and weary arms. Spring was moving in the air above and in the earth below and around him, penetrating even his dark and lowly little house with its spirit of divine discontent and longing. It was small wonder, then, that he suddenly flung down his brush on the floor, said 'Bother!' and 'O blow!' and also 'Hang spring-cleaning!' and bolted out of the house without even waiting to put on his coat. Something up above was calling him imperiously, and he made for the steep little tunnel which answered in his case to the gravelled carriage-drive owned by animals whose residences are nearer to the sun and air. So he scraped and scratched and scrabbled and

scrooged, and then he scrooged again and scrabbled and scratched and scraped, working busily with his little paws and muttering to himself, 'Up we go! Up we go!' till at last, pop! his snout came out into the sunlight, and he found himself rolling in the warm grass of a great meadow.

'This is fine!' he said to himself. 'This is better than whitewashing!' The sunshine struck hot on his fur, soft breezes caressed his heated brow, and after the seclusion of the cellarage he had lived in so long the carol of happy birds fell on his dulled hearing almost like a shout. Jumping off all his four legs at once, in the joy of living and the delight of spring without its cleaning, he pursued his way across the meadow till he reached the hedge on the further side.

'Hold up!' said an elderly rabbit at the gap. 'Sixpence for the privilege of passing by the private road!' He was bowled over in an instant by the impatient and contemptuous Mole, who

trotted along the side of the hedge chaffing the other rabbits as they peeped hurriedly from their holes to see what the row was about. 'Onion-sauce! Onion-sauce!' he remarked jeeringly, and was gone before they could think of a thoroughly satisfactory reply.

It all seemed too good to be true. Hither and thither through the meadows he rambled busily, along the hedgerows, across the copses, finding everywhere birds building, flowers budding, leaves thrusting – everything happy, and progressive, and occupied. And instead of having an uneasy conscience pricking him and whispering 'Whitewash!' he somehow could only feel how jolly it was to be the only idle dog among all these busy citizens. After all, the best part of a holiday is perhaps not so much to be resting yourself as to see all the other fellows busy working.

Kenneth Grahame
from The wind in the willows

The Voracious Vacuum Cleaner

There was an old woman who lived all alone in a bungalow. At times she wanted company and wondered if she should buy a cat or a dog. But she was a finicky old person who liked to keep her home spotlessly clean and she thought an animal would make it dirty.

One day the doorbell rang and there was a man standing on her doorstep holding a bulky parcel.

'Madam, allow me to show you our latest vacuum cleaner,' he said. 'It is called The Voracious. It will go anywhere, consume anything. It is much more use than a pet as it cleans up instead of messing everything. It doesn't need food either, just dust and rubbish.'

When he unpacked The Voracious, the old woman saw that it did indeed look rather like an unusual pet. It had a sleek grey body and a long hose coming out of one end that looked like a neck. When the man switched it on, it gave a low purr that sounded like, 'I'm hunngree.' The old woman was delighted. 'It even talks!' she said, 'I'll buy it.'

When the man had gone, she eagerly began to try out The Voracious. Soon there was not a speck of dust left, but The Voracious still purred: 'I'm hunngree, I'm hunngree.'

'You are a greedy one,' said the old woman affectionately. But as she turned round to find some more dust for it, there was a sound like 'SCHRULLP SCHRULLP,' and a rug whizzed into The Voracious Vacuum Cleaner's nozzle, quickly followed by some cushions, a small table and the television.

'Stop! Stop!' cried the old woman, but The Voracious just said, 'I'm hunngree, I'm hunngree.'

This time it sounded more like a snarl than a purr. Next the sofa and two armchairs disappeared down it with an even louder SCHRULLP. As the furniture went down, the hose bulged like a python swallowing a goat.

'Stop it at once!' shrieked the old woman, but as she stretched out to switch off The Voracious, SCHRULLPSCHRULLP, down she went too and landed with a bump on the sofa inside.

After all this eating, The Voracious had grown to about the size of a van, but it still went on gobbling everything it could see. When it had swallowed everything in the bungalow, it rolled into the street. There it met the milkman on his delivery round. He was carrying two crates of milk bottles. The Voracious was now the size of a truck and blocked the road. The milkman said, 'Please would you move out of the way.'

'I'm Hunngree Hunngree Hunngree!' growled The Voracious Vacuum Cleaner and SCHRULLP SCHRULLP SCHRULLP down went the milkman, milk crates and all.

'Pity you don't have any tea with you,' said the old woman, when the milkman and his bottles landed with a crash inside. 'I could do with a cup right now.'

By now The Voracious was the size of a bus. Round the corner came a class of schoolchildren with their teacher. They had been to the library and each clutched a book.

'Let the children pass,' cried the teacher!

'I'm HUNNGREE HUNNGREE HUNNGREE!' SCHRULLP SCHRULLP down went all the children and the teacher.

'Make yourselves comfortable and have some milk,' said the old woman and the milkman when the teacher and the children landed in a heap on the sofa.

Now The Voracious was as large as a cottage and it rolled into the High Street. Just then a crowd of young men going to a football match came face to face with it. They were dressed in bright hats and scarves and they were singing their team song. Before they could pause for breath The Voracious roared: 'I'M HUNNGREE HUNNGREE HUNNGREE!'

And SCHRULLP SCHRULLP SCHRULLP SCHRULLP down the hose they all went still singing, 'Here we go! Here we go! Here we go!'

'You can make yourselves useful and read to the children,' said the old woman, the milkman and the teacher when the football fans tumbled on to the sofa.

Next a great yellow crane came rumbling up the road. With it was a team of builders in yellow overalls and hard hats. They were on their way to a building site. The Voracious was now the size of a house. 'Move yourself, mate!' shouted the crane driver.'

'I'm HUNNGREE HUNNGREE HUNNGREE!' The Voracious bellowed, and SCHRULLP SCHRULLP SCHRULLP SCHRULLP down went the crane and the builders.

'Oh, we are glad to see you,' said the old woman, the milkman, the teacher, the children and the football fans when the crane and the builders squeezed in. 'Perhaps you'll be able to get us out of this monstrous machine.' But the crane driver and the builders had no better ideas than anyone else.

Meanwhile, the Voracious had grown to the size of a church, so it barely noticed a roller-skate lying lost in the road, though it swallowed it up all the same. But the skate had no intention of being swallowed right down inside The Voracious. Instead it rolled into the vacuum cleaner's machinery.

At that moment a big fire engine came screeching up the road, its sirens blaring. The Voracious swelled even larger and reached out its nozzle, but the only sound that came out was CLICKHISS CLICKHISS CLICKHISS CLUNK CLUNK. The roller skate had jammed the works. The body of The Voracious went on swelling as it tried to swallow until there was a loud BOOM!

There, sitting among the wreckage, were the old lady, the milkman, the teacher, the children, the football fans, the builders and the crane.

Everyone helped the old woman take her furniture back into her bungalow. She saw the roller skate glinting in the rubble and, thinking that it might come in useful, took it back as well.

It proved very useful indeed because after that the old woman did not like to use a vacuum cleaner. Instead, she scooted round the bungalow on the skate whenever she did her sweeping. This made it a much quicker job. And she was never lonely again because she had made so many friends inside The Voracious Vacuum Cleaner.

Laura Cecil
from The Voracious Vacuum Cleaner

Spring cleaning at home

Recycling their old possessions which are in good condition is a project the children could get involved with. It might also be possible to repair or refurbish some of those past their best. Toys, books, videotapes and so on could be donated to a charity shop or hospital. Alternatively they could be sold at a school fund-raising event or perhaps the school could take a communal stall at a boot fair, the proceeds going to a favourite charity. This encourages the children to clean their rooms and also helps to reduce the accumulation of waste.

Spring cleaning at school

1. You could organise a litter survey of the school. Groups of children with rubber gloves and rubbish bins can collect the litter from different areas in the school. Back in the classroom the types of litter can be categorised and litter 'hot spots' pinpointed. An anti-litter campaign can then be devised. As well as making and displaying posters in relevant places, the children might be able to suggest new sites for litter bins. If they survey the contents of the existing bins, they may well discover that some of them are hardly used because they are in the wrong place. Any anti-litter campaign should also include ideas for reducing the amount of waste created in the first place. There are a number of useful activity packs about waste and litter, including *The dustbin pack*, published by Waste Watch and available from The Department of Trade and Industry, The Environment Unit, Room 1016 Ashdown House, 123 Victoria Street, London SW1E 6RB.

2. The school could take an initiative in encouraging recycling. Organise a 'spring turn-out'. Old exercise books and used paper can be collected and taken to a recycling centre. Unwanted text books, library books or other school equipment in good condition can be donated to a charity which passes them on to schools in developing countries. Two you could contact are Ranfurly Library Service, 39–41 Coldharbour Lane, London SE5 9NR, tel: 071-733 3577 or Books for Development, 67 Lancaster Road, London N4 4PL, tel: 071-272 2206. For other items you could consult *Waste not*, a book containing hundreds of addresses of charities and what they collect. Available from Charities Aid Foundation, 48 Pembury Road, Tonbridge, Kent TN9 2JD. Tel: 0732 771333. A very good pack covering recycling and the school sur-

roundings amongst other topics, is *Green your school*, from Friends of the Earth, Education Section, 26-28 Underwood Street, London N1 7JQ.

Investigating natural recycling

Various creatures act as nature's cleaners. Birds and insects, particularly ants, are very efficient cleaners. In a corner of a school garden or other protected spot outside, place a piece of fruit core or vegetable stalk (a piece that humans do not usually eat) and get the children to observe it every day. They can chart the types of insects found on the item. These insects will be helping to break it down and will be recycling it. Record how long it takes to disappear completely. If a mould starts to grow, that should be recorded too.

Children can conduct a simple experiment to investigate which items commonly thrown away are biodegradable.

a) Collect some everyday items normally put in the rubbish bin, such as an apple core, potato peel, a slice of bread, a piece of newspaper, a piece cut from a plastic bottle, polystyrene, tin can, a piece cut from an ordinary plastic carrier bag and one from a 'biodegradable' one . . .

b) Dig a hole for each item, just deep enough to bury it.

c) Mark each spot and make a note of what it is and when it was buried.

d) Leave the items buried for a month or so, then check to see if they are still there. Some may have disappeared, others may be unchanged. Cover them up and try again in another month. When children have discovered which items do not degrade, they might devise a campaign to inform people of the hazards of using too many non-biodegradable objects.

❧ APRIL FOOLS' DAY

No one quite knows where the custom of playing April Fool jokes started, but there are a number of theories. It may go back to ancient times when the spring equinox was celebrated and people were glad to have some fun after the long winter. It has some similarities with the Hindu spring festival of Holi (see page 66).

One unlikely suggestion is that it commemorates the day that the dove Noah had sent out returned to the ark without finding land. Another idea is that on this day the court jester was given his only morning off, and ordinary people took over and played the fool. The idea of playing tricks on people seems to have started in France about 400 years ago. It could be related to the fact that in 1564 the French decided to change the date of the New Year from April 1st to January 1st. It had been the custom for people to exchange New Year gifts, so now some people exchanged mock presents on the date of the old New Year.

In France a customary trick is to pin a paper fish on someone's back without their knowing. When they discover it everyone shouts 'poisson d'avril'(April fish), the usual expression for an April Fool in France. From France the April Fool custom spread through Europe and to other parts of the world. In Scotland the expression was 'April gowk' (cuckoo). Certainly it was popular in England in the 18th century. Poor Robin's Almanac for 1760 has this rhyme:

The first of April some do say,
Is set apart for All Fools' Day.
But why the people call it so,
Nor I, nor they themselves do know.

On one famous occasion, a number of people turned up at the Tower of London after receiving invitations to see 'the annual ceremony of washing the white lions'. Nowadays in Britain, the newspapers, television and radio all join in, putting out spoof reports. A famous one was the television programme about workers in Italy harvesting spaghetti from trees.

Part of the tradition that is generally agreed on is that all jokes must stop at noon. If not the victim can reply with the age-old rhyme:

April Fools' Day's past and gone,
You're the Fool and I am none.

April 1st

You could
have fooled me.
The sun
came out
at playtime
then went
in again.

The wind
blew me off my bike.
It made my ears
ache!
It thrashed
the daffodils.
They looked bleak
and perished
their noses
to the ground.
And then it snowed.
Hard.

It's light later
though.
And time for play
after tea.
A blackbird sings.
He's a fool
as well.
He thinks
it's spring.

Ann Bonner

On April fools day when I went to school me and my friends decided to play a trick on our teacher. My friend had a bottle of clear nail polish so we covered a chalk in it. After play the teacher started to write on the blackboard and nothing happened so we all started to lagh and shouted April fool!!

Leela age 10

All Fools' Day

First voice:	Look you bicycle wheel turning round! When you look down you feel like a clown.
Chorus:	Yay, yay, Today is All Fools' Day!
Second voice:	Look you drop a penny pon the ground! When you think you lucky and look down, Not a thing like money pon the ground.
Chorus:	Yay, yay, Today is All Fools' Day!
Third voice:	Look you shoelace loose out! When you hear the shout and look down at you shoe It ain't true, it ain't true.
Chorus:	Yay, yay, Today is All Fools' Day!
Fourth voice:	Look you mother calling you! Look you mother calling you! Is true, is true, is true!
First voice:	Well let she call till she blue, I ain't going nowhay. You ain't ketching me this time Today is All Fools' Day.
Mother's voice:	Kenrick! Kenrick! Kenrrriicckk! See how long I calling this boy and he playing he ain't hear. When he come I gon cut he tail!

John Agard

 ## *Fools' errands*

It is a traditional trick to send someone on a silly errand, like going to fetch a tin of striped paint, a glass hammer for delicate nails, a left-handed cup, an elastic tape measure or – oldest of all perhaps – a tin of elbow grease. Nowadays, people also try to get others to make silly phone calls – asking for Mr Lion at the zoo or Ms Fish at the aquarium. Ask the children to make up their own fool's errand or silly phone calls and illustrate them with cartoons.

Song on May Morning

Now the bright morning Star, Dayes harbinger,
Comes dancing from the East, and leads with her
The Flowry May, who from her green lap throws
The yellow Cowslip and the pale Primrose.
   Hail, bounteous May, that dost inspire
   Mirth and youth and young desire,
Woods and Groves, are of thy dressing,
Hill and Dale doth boast thy blessing.
Thus we salute thee with our early Song,
And welcome thee, and wish thee long.

John Milton

 ## MAY DAY

For centuries May Day has been a time for celebration throughout northern Europe, and in Britain it used to be the high spot of the year. Many customs come from the Roman festival of Floralia, which was in honour of Flora, goddess of flowers. Others derive from the Celtic feast of Beltane, when all the fires were put out in people's homes and the hearth was swept. A big communal bonfire was lit and from this everyone would take a burning brand to light new fires at home. (This is similar to the tradition of the Paschal candle, see page 58.) It was considered lucky to jump over the Beltane fire.

In times past young people in Britain would 'go a-Maying'. Before dawn, they would collect boughs of greenery, often knots of hawthorn (hence 'nuts in May') which were carried back in procession. Often, in fact, the revels would start the night before and people would stay out all night. May Day itself was a festival full of fun, dancing and sporting competitions. Customs varied in different parts of the country, but there was nearly always a May Queen who presided over the celebration. Sometimes children made a kind of cage of garlands with a doll inside as a May Queen, and they would parade this round the village. The 'green man', a strange figure covered in leaves, also featured in many places. He had to die a symbolic death to represent the death of winter. A swordsman sometimes cleared away evil spirits.

The Puritans frowned on all such pagan revelry and forbade the celebrations. Now the church has taken over some aspects, with May carols at dawn from Magdalen College in Oxford and on the top of Bargate in Southampton, and the whole month being dedicated to Mary, mother of Jesus. Vestiges of the fun remain in some parts of the country, with fairs and parades still a May Day feature.

 ## THE MAYPOLE

The maypole was usually the centre of the May Day festivities, particularly the dancing. A straight tree was chosen and all but the topmost branch were stripped. This represented new growth. It was then decorated according to local custom – with ribbons, garlands, a crown, blown egg shells, painted stripes . . . In some villages, a permanent maypole was set up on the green. The maypole tradition probably came from pagan tree worship and, unlike many other traditions, did not become 'Christianised'. The Puritans banned them altogether, and there was much rejoicing on the first May Day after the Restoration. In London a 40 metre maypole was erected in the Strand after being floated down the Thames, accompanied by wild celebrations.

Dancing round the maypole involving plaiting the ribbons didn't start until the late eighteenth century and came from southern Europe. The colours of the ribbons are traditionally blue for the sky, yellow for the sun and green for new growth.

DANCING

Dancing has always been part of May Day celebrations and other May events. Many of the May Day dances were variations on what we now call Morris dancing, and were to do with encouraging the fertility of the land. The stamping feet, clashing sticks and bells on the legs were both to wake up the spirits in the ground and to frighten away evil spirits.

There are May dancing traditions still in parts of Britain, including the famous Furry dance in Helston, Cornwall. The name comes from the Latin *feria* – festival, or Celtic *feur* – holiday. The people of the town, dressed in their best clothes, the men traditionally in morning dress, dance sedately through the streets, in and out of houses, supposedly bringing good luck. Also in Cornwall, another dance involves the Padstow 'Oss. (Hobby horses were commonly associated with Morris dancing.) A man dressed in a black tarpaulin draped over a huge hoop, and with a fearsome mask, dances boisterously through the town.

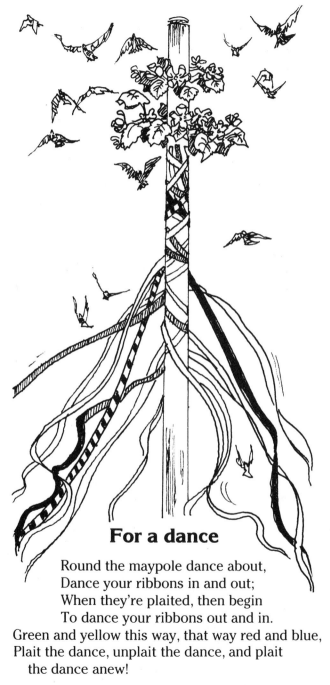

For a dance

Round the maypole dance about,
Dance your ribbons in and out;
When they're plaited, then begin
To dance your ribbons out and in.
Green and yellow this way, that way red and blue,
Plait the dance, unplait the dance, and plait
the dance anew!

Eleanor Farjeon

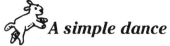

A simple dance

This dance might be used as part of a larger spring festival, or for a special May Day assembly. You will need around eight dancers and a bouquet of spring flowers. One child is chosen to lead the dance while the others sit in a well-spaced circle. The leader represents Spring and could be dressed accordingly in a green set of clothes, garlanded with flowers. Spring invites the other children to join the dance by offering each in turn the bouquet of flowers.

During part A of the music, Spring dances round the circle of children. At B, Spring stops in front of one of the children to present the bouquet.

A – to a count of 4, take three steps forward leading with the left foot, and on the last count hop with the left foot, raising the right foot in front – not behind. Bring the right foot down on the first of the next group of four counts so that this time the right foot leads and the left foot is raised in the hop.

B – to a count of 4, step with the left, hop with the left, step with the right, hop with the right. To the next four counts, bow on 1 and 2, present the bouquet on 3 and 4. The recipient repeats these movements, returning the bouquet to Spring.

A – Spring, followed by the first child chosen, dances round the circle again.

Continue the dance until all the children have formed a crocodile behind Spring. To close, the children form a dancing circle round Spring as music A is played. At B, Spring bows to the circle, and the circle bows to Spring.

Dawn Purkiss

L: left foot   R: right foot $\frac{L}{H}$: hop with left $\frac{R}{H}$: hop with right   *arranged by Timothy Roberts*

Spring cleaning rap

Well, we'll dust in the morning
 and through the night;
We'll make every corner
 look shiny and bright.
We can dust a little here,
 and dust a little there;
We can dust a little more,
 dust everywhere.
 When spring comes knocking at your door,
 Your house must be a-gleaming;
 So get your buckets, mops and brooms;
 It's time to start spring cleaning.

Well, we'll sweep all the carpets
 and make them gleam,
The old vacuum cleaner,
 he's getting up steam,
He can sweep a little here,
 and sweep a little there,
Sweep a little more,
 sweep everywhere.
 When spring comes knocking at your door . . .

Well, we'll clean all the cupboards
 and we'll clean the taps,
We'll clean all the chairs
 and we'll clean the cat,
We can clean a little here,
 and clean a little there,
Clean a little more,
 clean everywhere.
 When spring comes knocking at your door . . .

Words and music by Niki Davies

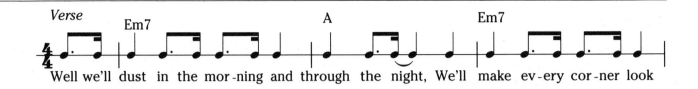

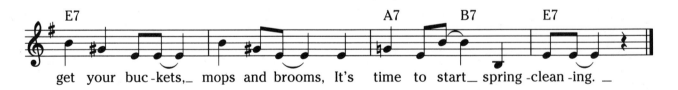

Build up a rhythmic background of spring cleaning sounds using real and improvised instruments – sandpaper blocks, rattles, scrubbing brushes, carpet beater, a vacuum cleaner, and so on. Emphasise the main beat as well as ostinato patterns from the rap:

Put on an action-packed spring cleaning performance based round the rap. The children could devise actions to fit the rhythm – scrubbing, sweeping, dusting – and choreograph a dance to perform while another group provides the music.

April fool

Dad's turned into Batman,
Did you see him flying off?
And be careful not to make a noise,
There's a monster in the loft.
    April fool, April fool;
    Has anyone got a leg to pull.
    It could be me it could be you;
    April fool.

There's a walrus in the bath tub,
He's feeling quite at home,
And you'd better come here quickly
'Cause the Queen is on the phone.
    April fool, April fool . . .

A Martian's at the corner shop
Buying tins of beans,
If you eat this daffodil
Then you could have nice dreams.
    April fool, April fool . . .

Words and music by Niki Davies

Easter

For Easter

On Easter Day in the morning the door of
  Heaven stands wide,
On Easter Day in the morning the angels
  wait outside,
The angels in their garments with sheaves
  of silver palms
They wait till Love rise up from earth to beg
  for Heaven's alms.
    On Easter Day in the morning,
    On Easter Day in the morning,
On Easter Day in the morning Love shall rise
  again,
He shall come to the door of Heaven and beg
  a boon for men.

Eleanor Farjeon

The first Easter

About 2000 years ago, a man called Jesus began
to talk to people about how they might lead
better lives, and he also cured many who were
ill or disabled. Crowds flocked to hear and see
this kind and gentle man, and from them he
chose twelve men to be his closest followers.

For about three years Jesus preached and
healed. It was in the Jewish scriptures that one
day a man would come who would save the
Jewish nation, and now some people believed
that Jesus was this saviour. The priests and
other leaders didn't like this, nor the fact that
Jesus seemed to break some of the strict
religious laws. They were envious of the great
following that Jesus had and were afraid of
losing their power. They decided they must
have him killed. One of Jesus's disciples, Judas,
agreed to help them for a payment of thirty
pieces of silver.

It was the time of year when Jews celebrated
Passover. Jesus and the disciples all sat down
together at what is now often known as The Last
Supper. Jesus shared the bread and wine with
the disciples and told them to do the same in
the future as a way of remembering him.

After the meal, they went to a quiet garden.
Jesus took three disciples a little apart from the
others and asked them to watch with him while
he prayed. He walked on a little and then prayed
to God to spare him the coming agony, but he
also said that he would accept whatever
happened if it were God's will. He returned to
find the three disciples could not keep awake
even in his time of great need. He woke them,
but the same thing happened three times.

Suddenly a crowd armed with swords and
sticks broke the quiet of the night. They had
been sent by the priests and elders to seize
Jesus, and with them was Judas. He went
straight to Jesus and said, 'Hail, Master,' and

kissed his cheek. This was the signal to the soldiers and they rushed forward. Jesus gave himself up peacefully but some of the disciples starting fighting until Jesus forbade them. As he was taken away, the disciples all fled because they were afraid they too would be seized.

Jesus was taken before the high priest and elders to be judged. They could find no real evidence against him, so they got some people to tell lies about the things he had said and accused him of blasphemy – speaking against God and the Jewish religion. This made the crowd very angry.

At this time the Romans were in power in Jerusalem, and the Jewish leaders had to get the agreement of the governor, Pontius Pilate, for Jesus to be killed. They told more lies about him, saying that he had claimed to be the king of the Jews and that he had tried to persuade people not to pay their taxes. When Pilate questioned Jesus, however, he could not find anything wrong and said he was innocent.

It was the custom at Passover for the Roman governor to release a prisoner from jail. Pilate knew there was a convicted murderer called Barabbas and he asked the crowd,

'Who do you want released, Jesus or Barabbas?' To Pilate's dismay, they shouted,

'Barabbas!'

Pilate tried to persuade them to change their minds, but without success. 'Well, what do you want me to do with Jesus?' he asked and the cry went up,

'Crucify him!'

With great reluctance the governor handed Jesus over to the soldiers and he was taken away and whipped. The soldiers made great fun of him, dressing him as a king with a crown made from thorn branches and taunting him by calling him 'King of the Jews'. Jesus was then taken with two criminals from the jail to a hill where all three were nailed to wooden crosses, a common form of execution in those days.

Even then the punishment was not over. Jesus was given vinegar to drink, the soldiers took his clothes and drew lots for them, and as people passed by they all mocked him:

'Call yourself the Son of God? Why don't you get Him to save you then?'

'If you come down off the cross, then we'll believe in you!'

Later, a great darkness covered the land, and after three hours Jesus died, asking God to forgive his enemies. A violent earthquake followed, making many people, including the chief soldier on guard, believe that Jesus really was the Son of God.

Jesus's body was taken down and put in a tomb. A great stone was rolled in front. The priests were afraid that the disciples would steal the body and tell people that Jesus had risen from the dead as he had foretold, so a guard was set to watch over it.

However, when some women followers of Jesus came to the tomb after two days, they found the stone rolled away and the tomb empty. They were very frightened, but an angel appeared and said,

'Don't be afraid. Jesus is no longer here. He is risen.'

The women were amazed but they went joyfully to tell the disciples the good news. Soon, Jesus appeared to them and in the weeks that followed he came to them several times and told them to continue his good works and spread his teachings of love and hope. This was how the Christian Church was born.

retold by Jill Brand

 **THE ROYAL MAUNDY MONEY**

The day before Good Friday is called 'Maundy' Thursday, which comes from the Latin *Mandatum novum da vobis* – 'A new commandment I give to you, (that ye love one another).' Jesus said this to his disciples at the Last Supper as he washed their feet. In the early days of the church priests and bishops would wash the feet of some of the poor people of the parish at a special service. Later, it became the custom for the monarch to do it. Henry VIII, for example, washed the feet of as many poor men as he was years old, and also gave them gifts. Queen Elizabeth continued the custom, but insisted that the feet were already well-washed first! The tradition stopped in 1754, but the money continued to be distributed. Nowadays special Maundy money, small silver coins, is minted. The Queen gives this to as many men and women as her age at a special ceremony, usually in Westminster Abbey.

THE PASCHAL CANDLE

In many churches a huge candle is lit on Easter Saturday, after the church has been made completely dark. The custom comes from pre-Christian days when huge bonfires were lit to dispel winter and welcome spring. Christians regard the candle as a symbol of Christ as the light of the world, and it also reminds them of the times He appeared to the disciples after the Resurrection. The candle is supposed to burn for the forty days until Ascension day. Traditionally people light their own smaller candles from it and, in times past, they would take these candles home to light a new fire in their hearth. The word 'Paschal' comes from 'Pesach', the Hebrew word for Passover.

EASTER PLAYS

The tradition of performing plays at Easter depicting the last days of Jesus goes back a long way throughout Europe. (The famous Oberammergau Passion Play used to be held at Easter, but changed to the summer for convenience.) In the Middle Ages there were very often elaborate pageants in churches, with fantastic costumes and scenery. Mummers' plays were also traditional in some places, a custom which still remains in some parts of Britain. In a number of villages in Yorkshire, for example, the story of St George and the Dragon, the triumph of good over evil, is acted out by local people.

EASTER PLANT LORE

Good Friday used to be one of the few holiday days and was, therefore, the first day that many working people could begin to get gardening done. In Devon, anything planted on Good Friday is said to 'grow goody'.

The value of Easter fires was another important feature of garden folk lore. Charred sticks from Easter Saturday's 'Burning of Judas' bonfires were buried in the soil to save crops from hail. The ashes of oak, beech and walnut trees charred in the sacred Easter fire then mixed with seeds promoted fertility.

Maundy Thursday is traditionally the best time for planting potatoes.

If it rains on Easter Day
There shall be good grass but very bad hay.

HOT CROSS BUNS

Hot cross buns are traditionally eaten on Good Friday, but these spiced buns pre-date the Christian festival. In earlier times it was thought that the bun represented the moon and the cross dividing it represented the four quarters of the moon. The Anglo-Saxons made small cakes marked with a cross to honour the goddess Diana at the spring festival. Before that, the Romans also ate spiced buns as a celebration of the coming of spring.

There are lots of superstitions surrounding hot cross buns. It was once believed that the buns baked early on Good Friday would have special powers. If they were overcooked and allowed to harden they could be kept for a year without going mouldy. These buns would then be used to try to cure common illnesses like dysentry and whooping cough.

Sailors thought that if they took a hot cross bun to sea with them it would safeguard them from shipwreck and they would return home safely.

It is thought that the rhyme 'Hot cross buns' was an advertising cry from the time when bakers sold their wares in the street.

Recipe for hot cross buns

Ingredients

The following quantities will make about 24 buns or more if they are not too big.

1 kg plain flour
5 ml (1 teaspoonful) salt
10 ml (2 teaspoonfuls) mixed spice
125 g butter or margarine
250 g currants
125 g caster sugar
2 × 7 g packets instant yeast
550 ml warm milk
2 eggs
a little extra milk and sugar for glazing at the end

Utensils

scales
measuring jug
large mixing bowl
smaller mixing bowl
wooden spoon
clean cloth
baking trays
knife
pastry brush

What to do

1 Mix together the flour, salt and spices in a large mixing bowl.

2 Cut the butter or margarine in small pieces, then rub it in with fingertips till the mixture is like fine crumbs.

3 Mix in the sugar and the fruit.

4 Stir the yeast and milk together in another bowl.

5 Beat the egg into the yeast liquid.

6 Make a well in the middle of the dry ingredients and pour the yeast liquid into it.

7 Mix well until a soft dough is formed.

8 Cover with a clean cloth and leave in a warm place for half an hour.

9 Grease the baking trays. (You can wipe them over with the greasy side of the butter or margarine paper.)

10 Divide up the mixture and shape into buns. Put them on the baking trays about 8 cm apart.

11 Leave them to rise again for about another half-hour. After about 20 minutes set the oven to 425°F, 220°C, gas mark 7.

12 Cut a cross in the top of each bun with the back of a knife.

13 Put them in the oven and bake for about 15-20 minutes.

14 When cooked, brush the buns with the milk and sugar and return them to oven for a couple of minutes to dry.

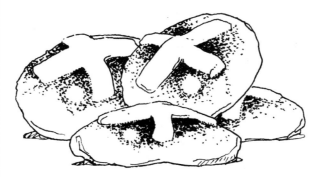

THE EASTER HARE

The hare has been associated with Easter for a very long time. It probably goes back to pre-Christian times when a hare was sacrificed to Eostre, goddess of spring (from whom we get the name of the festival). Certainly spring is the time of year when hares are most often seen. It is said that if a hare is being hunted, another will take its place when it is tired, and this may be one reason why it has been adopted as an appropriate Easter symbol, Jesus having died to save sinners.

The Easter Hare

Long, long ago there was a village where the people were very poor. One Easter-time the mothers had no money to buy the presents of sweets they usually gave to their children on Easter Sunday. They were very sad for they knew how disappointed the children would be.

'What shall we do?' they asked each other, as they drew water from the well.

'We have plenty of eggs,' sighed one.

'The children are tired of eggs,' said another.

Then one of the mothers had an idea, and before dinner-time all the mothers in the village knew about it, but not a single child.

Early on Easter morning, the mothers left their homes and went into the woods with little baskets on their arms. It was quite impossible to see what they had in the baskets as they were covered with coloured cloths. When the mothers returned home, the cloths were tied about their heads like head-squares and the baskets were filled with wild flowers.

'My mother went to pick flowers for Easter this morning,' said one child, as they all walked together to church.

'So did mine!' said another.

'And mine too!' said all the others, and laughed for they were happy and it was Easter Sunday.

When they came out of church, the children were told to go and play in the woods before dinner. Off they ran, laughing and talking. Suddenly someone shouted, 'Look what I've found!'

'A RED egg!'

'I've found a BLUE one!'

'Here's a nest full! All different colours!'

They ran about searching in the bushes and filling their pockets and hats.

'What kind of eggs are they?' they asked each other.

'They're too big for wild birds' eggs.'

'They're the same size as hens' eggs!'

'Hens don't lay eggs these bright colours, silly!' Just then a hare ran out from behind a bush.

'They're hares' eggs!' cried the children. 'The hare laid the eggs! The hare laid the eggs! Hurrah for the Easter hare!'

German legend
retold by Norah Montgomerie

THE ORIGIN OF EASTER EGGS

From far back in history eggs have been a symbol of new life. Many creation myths feature an egg as the beginning of all things. (See, for example, the story on page 19.) It was a tradition in both Ancient Egypt and Persia for friends to give each other dyed eggs in springtime, and the early Christians adopted it as a particularly appropriate Easter custom. As well as representing the Resurrection and the new life and hope which Jesus brought to the world, the egg itself is rather like the tomb from which He rose from the dead.

Eggs acquired added significance because, at one time, they were one of the foods banned during Lent, so Easter Sunday was the first day for six weeks when they could be eaten.

DECORATED EGGS

Throughout Europe and the Middle East there are various traditions for decorating eggs. Greek and Syrian Christians give each other red eggs in honour of the blood of Christ. In central Europe, eggs are decorated with delicate and intricate designs using a method similar to batik cloth dying. In Austria, a pattern is often achieved by tying tiny plants round the eggs before boiling them. Painted pictures, gold, silver and even jewels have been used. Edward 1 of England was reported to have given over 400 decorated eggs to his household. Some were dyed, but for the more fortunate, some eggs were covered with gold leaf.

Making decorated eggs

There are many ways eggs can be decorated in school. For young children it is probably better if you hardboil the eggs first, as empty shells may be too fragile for them to hold and work on. In fact, if eggs are boiled very hard, they will keep for years.

Older children can use blown egg shells. Wash the shells thoroughly then make a small hole at one end of the egg and a larger one at the other.

'Jewelled' eggs can be made by first dyeing or painting the shells then, using PVA adhesive, sticking on sequins, gummed stars, beads, present-wrapping ribbon, Lurex thread and other shiny trimmings. This can be quite delicate work requiring patience to allow time for the glue to set. Cocktail sticks are useful for holding beads and sequins in place while the glue dries.

The point of a thin metal skewer heated to red hot in a flame is the easiest way, but probably shouldn't be attempted by the children. Holding the egg so that the holes are covered, shake it to break the yolk. Hold it over a bowl and blow gently into the smaller hole so that the contents come out. Rinse out the inside with water.

If you want to dye eggs, the best way is to buy the special dye, often obtainable from shops selling Greek foods. You can also use cochineal, but other food colourings are not always so successful. To avoid disappointing the children, you could experiment with them first at home.

Designs can be drawn on with felt-tipped pens or, for really special effects, gold and silver pens. It is easier to draw designs with curved lines than straight ones. Encourage the children to plan and practise their patterns on paper first. Designs can be abstract, or they can incorporate leaves, flowers or other pictures. Oil paints also work very successfully on egg shells. If the children are using blown eggs, they can be hung up, perhaps on a classroom 'Easter tree', made from a bare branch. Thread a long darning needle with coloured thread, tie a bead to one end, and carefully thread the needle through the holes in the egg.

EASTER EGG CUSTOMS

In a number of places in Britain rolling hardboiled, painted eggs downhill is an Easter Monday custom. It has become a competition between children, to see which egg travels furthest.

In Ireland, children make a nest from little stones on Palm Sunday. In them they place duck and goose eggs which they collect throughout Holy Week. These are shared with others on Easter Sunday.

In parts of Germany, empty eggshells are used to decorate trees and shrubs during Easter week.

In North America parents hide chocolate eggs around the house or garden and the children have to hunt for them.

In parts of Greece, it is the custom to place a red egg on a loved one's grave at Easter.

THE EASTER CHICK

The chick has become associated with Easter because it is what comes from the egg – another symbol of new life. The chick emerges from the seemingly lifeless egg as Jesus emerged from the tomb. It is also a symbol of the cycle of life – egg, chick, hen, egg.

Making an Easter chick

You will need:

a cleaned-out egg shell
yellow wool
thin card
white gummed paper
orange card or paper

What to do

1 Cut two circles with a diameter of 6 cm out of thin card. Cut a hole in the centre of each with a diameter of 3 cm.
2 Place the rings together and wind wool round and round until the central hole is almost filled.

3 Snip the wool all round the circumference and tie a length of wool tightly round the middle, between the two card circles.

4 Gently pull the card circles off and fluff up the wool to make a pom pom.
5 Make the eyes by cutting out two small circles of white gummed paper and stick them on.
6 Cut out a beak from the orange paper or card and glue on, or fasten with a couple of stitches.
7 Put the chick in the egg shell.

The completed chicks in their shells can be put in egg cartons, or children could make a nest from Plasticene, papier mâché, clay or card, padded with tissue paper.

Chicks can also be made with two pom poms, one for the head and a larger one for the body. Feet and wings could be made from card and stitched on.

Hare and the Easter egg

Hare gave a chirrup of joy when he saw that the shop was still open. Brushes hung at the door and jars of sweets in the window shone with many colours in the dim light of the lamp.

Hare crept close. It was a lovely sight! Whips and tops, dolls and toy horses, cakes and buns were there.

Then he opened his eyes very wide, for he saw something strange in the medley of toys and food. On a dish lay a pile of chocolate eggs with sugary flowers and 'Happy Easter' written upon them. Ribbons were tied round them in blue, pink and yellow bows.

'Eggs! 'Normous eggs! Eggs brown as earth. Beautiful eggs!' whispered Hare.

He stared and licked his lips.

'What kind of hen lays these pretty eggs? Ribbons on 'em! What would Grey Rabbit say? I should like to take her one and Squirrel one and me one.'

He pressed closer to the glass and his long ears flapped against the pane. Then footsteps came down the street and he slipped into the shadows and crouched there dark as night.

A woman stopped at the shop window. She smiled when she saw the Easter eggs. She lifted the door latch and pushed open the door. A loud tinkle-tinkle came from the bell hanging above it.

'Good evening, Mrs Bunting,' called the woman.

'Good evening, Mrs Snowball,' replied Mrs Bunting.

'Those are nice Easter eggs, Mrs Bunting,' said Mrs Snowball. 'How much are they?'

'A shilling each,' replied Mrs Bunting, and she reached the dish from the window.

Hare crept into the shop and stood by Mrs Snowball's skirts.

Mrs Snowball chose her egg and while the two women chatted, Hare moved round. He stretched out a furry paw, he took a leap, and he snatched a chocolate egg. In a moment he was gone, out into the dusk.

'Oh! Oh!' cried Mrs Bunting. 'What was that?'

'I didn't see anything,' said Mrs Snowball. 'Was it a cat?'

They both ran to the shop door, but Hare was already far away, running like the wind.

'You can't catch me,' laughed Hare, capering along the fields, and he squeezed the egg under his arm. Then he stopped to look at it. His warm fur had softened the chocolate and his fist went through. He brought out a fluffy chicken made of silk and wool.

'Not real, but a good pretence,' said Hare. He licked his paws and then licked the egg.

'Oh! 'Larcious! De-larcious!' he cried, and soon the egg disappeared.

'That's the best egg I've ever tasted,' said he, and he galloped across the common and dashed into the little house where Grey Rabbit was cooking the supper. Squirrel sat there making the toast.

'Here you come at last, Hare,' cried Squirrel. 'What have you been eating? You are brown and dirty.'

'Not dirt, Squirrel. It's chocolate. I've eaten an egg laid by an Easter hen and it was made of chocolate,' said Hare proudly.

'Chocolate egg?' cried Grey Rabbit. 'Where was it?'

'In the village shop,' said Hare. 'I took it right under the nose of Mrs Bunting.'

'Hare! You stole it!' cried Grey Rabbit.

'I shall go and pay for it,' explained Hare. 'It was a shilling.'

'You took an egg and you ate it all yourself,' said Squirrel. 'Greedy Hare!'

'I brought you the ribbon, Squirrel, and the little fluffy chicken inside the egg is for Grey Rabbit,' said Hare, bringing the ribbon and the chicken from his pocket.

'And did an Easter hen lay these?' they asked.

All evening they talked of Easter eggs, and the next morning Squirrel spoke to Old Hedgehog when he came with the milk.

'Have you ever seen an Easter egg, Hedgehog?'

Hedgehog set down his pails.

'I don't know what it is,' said he. 'You'd best ask Wise Owl.'

After breakfast the three locked the door and set off for Wise Owl's house. They rang the little silver bell and they stood in a row under the tree waiting for him.

'Who's there?' hooted Wise Owl very crossly. 'Go away or I'll eat you.'

'Please, Wise Owl. . .' began Grey Rabbit, waving her handkerchief for a truce.

'We want to know. . .' added Squirrel, stammering with fright.

'About Easter Eggs,' shouted Hare in a loud voice.

'I've a good mind to tell you nothing,' said Wise Owl frowning at the noisy Hare.

'Yes, Wise Owl,' said Grey Rabbit meekly.

'Easter eggs come at Easter,' said Wise Owl. 'The church bells ring, and the little birds sing, and the sun dances on Easter morning.'

He blinked and yawned and went to bed, banging his door so that the bough shook.

'He won't tell us any more,' said Grey Rabbit. 'Let us go away quickly before he eats us.'

Alison Uttley
from Hare and the Easter egg

PARADES AND BONNETS

This is not a very old tradition, although the idea of having new clothes at Easter is quite ancient and wide-spread. The idea for the big parade in Battersea Park in London arose from an incident in 1829. A duel was fought between two noblemen and, far from being a secret, huge crowds of London's fashionable society came to watch. Another big occasion for showing off their new clothes came twenty years later when Queen Victoria visited the newly renovated park at Easter. Gradually it became an annual custom for people to parade in the park at Easter, displaying their fine new clothes. The women's hats became a particular focus as hats were extremmely decorative in Victorian times.

Nowadays, there is a big parade, with floats and marching bands, and the Easter bonnet tradition is found throughout the country.

 *Making Easter bonnets*

You will need:

2 large pieces of card
scissors
crêpe paper, tissue paper or other decorations of your choice
stapler or sticky tape
glue

What to do

1 Cut a strip of card long enough to go all the way round the head. This band will be the crown of the hat and can be as tall as you like.

2 Fit it to the head and secure the ends.

3 Place this headband on the second sheet of card and draw round it. Draw another, larger circle round it for the brim of the hat. This can be as wide as you like. Cut round the large circle.

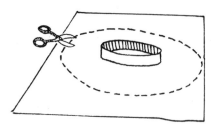

4 Make a hole in the centre of the circle and cut outwards to the circumference of the inner circle making a number of triangles. Bend these triangles back so they stand upright.

5 Place the band on the hat brim so that the upright tabs are inside it. Stick the tabs to the inside of the band.

6 Decorate the hat with crêpe paper bows, paper doilies for a lace effect, tissue paper flowers, Easter chicks. . . Add ribbon or crêpe paper ties if you wish.

Easter round

Every girl and every boy,
Raise your voices, sing for joy,
Christ is ris'n at Eastertide.

Words and music by Veronica Clark

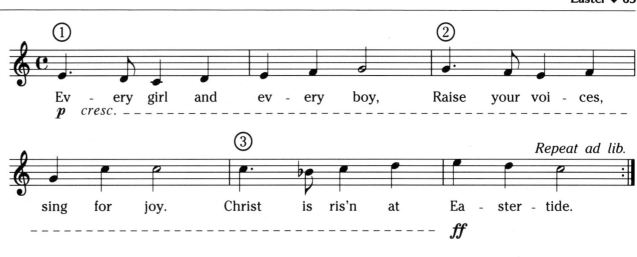

Ev - ery girl and ev - ery boy, Raise your voi - ces,
p *cresc.*

sing for joy. Christ is ris'n at Ea - ster - tide.
ff

Repeat ad lib.

Voice 1, soprano xylophone

Ha-le-lu-ja, praise the Lord.

Voice 2, glockenspiel

Ha-le-lu - ja.

Voice 3, bass xylophone

Ha - le - lu - ja.

Simple ostinato piano accompaniment

(p)

The effect of this simple round should be of a gradual, joyful crescendo as each new vocal or instrumental part enters.

More spring festivals

HOLI

Holi is an important festival celebrated by Hindus all over the world. It is a time for singing and dancing, for fun and mischief. It is a festival of colour, when people spray each other, friends or complete strangers, with coloured water with no possible recriminations.

Holi is a festival of spring which symbolises the time of fertility, new life and growth. In the countryside the farmers celebrate it as the time to harvest their winter crops. According to some Indian astrological calendars, Holi is considered to be the start of the New Year.

The festival has religious and mythological associations. It is believed that Lord Krishna played mischievous tricks upon the *Gopis* (dairy maids) and the cowherds at this time and that they sprayed each other with red paint. It is also associated with the marriage of Lord Shiva when the onlookers honoured him by covering themselves in bright colours and by singing and

dancing. The spraying of coloured water is a re-creation of the wedding procession.

Before Holi can be celebrated certain preparations have to be made. The whole house is cleaned thoroughly and rangoli patterns are drawn outside the house by the front door. Sometimes the patterns are made with rice and coloured spices, such as turmeric and chilli powder, and sometimes a rice paste is used. Less traditionally, the patterns are made from coloured chalk or powder paint.

On the evening before Holi, bonfires are lit all over India to symbolise the burning of the demoness Holika. One story tells how Holika tried to kill the Lord Krishna by burning down his house. Lord Krishna got to hear of her plan and, as she tried to carry it out, he surprised her and reversed the action, setting her alight. He escaped while she burned to death.

Holi – festival of spring

I cannot tell you how much I looked forward to Holi. In fact, I longed for it a good three hundred and sixty-four days of the year. The reason was that our family did such unusual things to celebrate Holi.

First of all, on the day of the full moon around late February or early March, we built a huge bonfire. This was called 'burning Holi', because on this day, ages ago, a wicked princess, Holika, was consumed by flames that she had intended for her innocent nephew Prahlad.

Frankly, I cared less for Holika, who was burnt in ancient history, than I did for the stuff we actually threw into our own bonfire. We threw whole sheaves of green wheat, whole bundles of green chickpeas, still on their stalks, pinecones filled with strategically hidden pinenuts, and then watched them as their skins got charred.

Only the outside skins were allowed to burn. That was the trick. Each one of us then used a stick to pull out whatever we wanted to eat. My favourite was the chickpeas – tiny chickpeas still in their green skins. Of course, the skins would turn brownish-black but the peas themselves would be deliciously roasted. Everything would be hot – we would almost burn our fingers trying to peel the chickpeas and remove the shells from the pinenuts. Their taste would have to last us for the rest of the year as we licked our lips and remembered.

By the end of it all, our faces were black and our clothes and hands were sooty, but no one seemed to mind, even our parents.

The funny thing about Holi was that we could 'burn' it one night and 'play' it the next morning. While the 'burning' had to do, naturally, with fire, the 'playing' had to do with water and colours. . . . As the Spring Festival approached, an army of us young cousins would, in great secrecy and in competing groups, begin its preparation of colours. . . .

Holi is a leveller, and there was no one we wanted to level more than those against whom we held grudges. A special ugly colour was prepared for them.

First we would go to the garage and call on one of the chauffeurs. 'Massoom Ali? Massoom Ali?' we would call.

Massoom Ali would poke his head out from the pit under the gleaming Ford. 'I am busy. Why are you children always disturbing me? Always coming here to eat my head. Barrister Sa'ab, your grandfather, wants the car at noon and I still have much work to do.'

'Just give us some of the dirtiest grease from under the car.'

'So, Holi is upon us again? Why don't you children use the normal red, green and yellow colours?'

'If you give us the grease, we won't spray you with the awful magenta paint we have prepared in the garden watertank. It is a fast colour, too.'

'Threatening an old man, are you! All right, all right. Just don't eat my head.'

The grease would be combined with mud, slime and permanent purple dye. The concoction would be reserved for the lowliest enemies. Elderly relatives got a sampling of the more dignified, store-bought powders, yellow, red and green. For our best friends, we prepared a golden paint, carefully mixing real gilt and oil in a small jar. This expensive colour, would, as I grew older, be saved only for those members of the opposite sex on whom I had the severest crushes – transforming them, with one swift application, into golden gods.

Madhur Jaffrey
from Seasons of splendour

The wicked king

This story gives a different version of the burning of Holika.

King Hiranya Kashyap was informed by a sage that he could not be killed by a man, a beast or a weapon, during the day or night, on earth or in water, inside or outside a house. His sister, Holika, was told that she could not be killed by fire.

This prophecy convinced them that they were immortal and soon they came to believe that they were gods. Everyone was forced to worship them. However, the king's son, Prahlad, refused to recognise them as gods, and the king in his fury ordered his servants to kill the boy. Each time they tried Prahlad was saved by God. Eventually King Hiranya Kashyap asked Holika to take his son into the middle of a giant bonfire and hold him there until he died. This she agreed to do, safe in the knowledge that she could not herself be burned. But while they were waiting in the flames she had a sudden change of heart and asked the gods to exchange Prahlad's life for hers. This they agreed to and the boy walked out unharmed.

When the king heard that his son was still alive he decided to kill Prahlad himself. The boy was chained to a pillar and the king raised his sword to strike. Suddenly, there was a tremendous clap of thunder and the pillar broke in two. From out of the pillar came God, in a strange and terrifying shape. He was half man and half beast. The top part of his body was that of a lion and the bottom part was that of a man. He picked up the king and carried him to the threshold of the palace and there placed him across his lap. By this time it was dusk. With one huge swipe of his long lion's claw he killed Hiranya Kashyap.

The prophecy had been proved right. The arrogant and cruel king had been killed, but by someone who was neither man nor beast; neither in a house nor outside it; not on earth nor in water; not during the day nor night; and no weapon had been used.

On the death of his father, Prahlad was proclaimed King and he ruled justly and well.

Holi

Under the full spring moon
Lord Krishna
watched young Rahda,
her downy beauty
delicate as pollen in the air,

a slim girl
in the slender light.

Krishna threw powder,
coloured powder
soft and mischievous as love
under the liquid moon;

through shadowed veils
her eyes danced.

New flowers bloomed
next day in Krishna's garden,
frail graceful girls
dancing their stories
to the powdered bees.

Irene Rawnsley

 **JAPANESE SPRING FESTIVALS**

In Japan, there are a number of festivals which occur in springtime. Japanese Buddhists celebrate the birth of the Lord Buddha by bathing statues of him with hydrangea leaf tea. The Cherry Blossom festival is a time for picnics in the park. An important celebration is Setsubun, which means 'change of season'. There are ceremonies in the temples and in people's homes. One tradition is to scatter roast beans in the home and also to throw them in the street. This symbolises driving away evil spirits, and is a reminder about making a fresh start.

Another custom which may have its origins in keeping away evil spirits is the Hina Doll festival. Japanese parents will usually present a daughter with a special set of dolls at her birth or on her first birthday. She will keep the dolls all her life. They represent the Emperor, Empress, attendants and musicians, and they are dressed in beautiful traditional clothes. Towards the end of February, they are displayed on a tiered stand, and the festival itself is on the 3rd March. There is festive food – diamond-shaped rice cakes and rice wine – and best kimonos are worn.

A festival for families with boys also takes place in spring, on 5th May. Again, dolls are displayed, but this time, warriors, and again, there is a special family meal. It is customary for the family to fly streamers in the shape of carp outside the house. In Japan, the carp is a symbol of courage and ambition.

 ***Kirigami***

The Japanese are famous for their skills in making things from paper. Kirigami is a form of paper cutting used to make blossoms symbolic of the coming of spring – traditionally plum, cherry and iris. Children's writing and other work about spring mounted on the wall can be decorated with cut-out paper flowers. Plum and cherry are easy shapes with five petals, but children may need a template for irises. They can also make other flowers – daffodils with trumpets made from single segments of egg cartons, for example.

Cut the iris shape out of folded paper.

The completed flower.

The Doll Festival
(haiku)

Lighted lanterns
cast a gentle radiance
on pink peach blossoms.

Third day of third month.
Mother brings out five long shelves –
black lacquer, red silk.

On the topmost shelf
we place gilded folding screens
and the two chief dolls.

They are Emperor
and Empress, in formal robes:
gauzes, silks, brocades.

On the lower steps,
court ladies with banquet trays,
samisen players.

High officials, too,
kneeling in solemn stillness:
young noble pages.

Fairy furniture –
dressers, mirrors, lacquer bowls,
bonsai, fans, braziers.

Should the royal pair
wish to go blossom-viewing –
two golden palanquins.

Third day of third month.
Our small house holds a palace –
we are its guardians.

Lighted lanterns
cast a gentle radiance
on pink peach blossoms.

James Kirkup

BAISAKHI

In April Sikhs celebrate the festival of Baisakhi. It is a spring and new year festival, coinciding with the beginning of the Indian calendar and marking the beginning of the spring harvest.

Baisakhi is particularly important because it reminds Sikhs of how their tenth Guru, Gobind Singh, brought together the faithful and formed the Sikh brotherhood. This is known as the *Khalsa* (the pure ones). To become a member of the Khalsa Sikhs have to go through the Amrit ceremony at the *gurdwara* (temple). When they have been baptised into the brotherhood they have to wear the five Ks. These are the *Kesh* (long hair), *Khanga* (comb which holds up the hair), the *Kara* (steel bracelet), the *Kirpan* (dagger) and *Kaccha* (loose underpants).

The forming of the Khalsa

In 1699, Guru Gobind Singh was at a great gathering of Sikhs and he decided to test their faith. He asked the crowd if there was anyone willing to die for his belief. The crowd fell silent until one man stood up and volunteered. Guru Gobind Singh led the man into a tent and then reappeared with a sword dripping with blood. He held up the sword to show the waiting crowd. Four times more he asked for a volunteer and took the men who came forward into the tent. Each time he appeared with the bloodstained sword. The five volunteers later emerged unharmed. Guru Gobind Singh had used animal blood on the sword.

The five men willing to become martyrs became known as the *panj pyare* (five brothers) and the first of the Khalsa.

 ### Finding out about Sikhism

With the children, research the history of Sikhism. When and where did it start?

Arrange for a Sikh from the local community to come in and talk with the children, and encourage any Sikh children in your class to share their experiences. It might be possible to arrange a visit to a gurdwara.

 ### The meaning of names

All Sikhs have a special name. Men usually use the name Singh, meaning lion, as a middle name, and women use Kaur, which means princess. List the names of all the children in the class and see if they can find out their origins, and whether they have a meaning. Children can ask at home why their names and others in the family were chosen.

They could make graphs showing the popularity of names within the school. Discuss names which are common to specific countries, cultures and religions. Both given and family names could be investigated.

Investigating symbols

Most religions have their own symbol. This is the *Khanda*, the symbol of Sikhism.

The double-edged sword symbolises the true knowledge which is needed in the battle against ignorance. The circle around the sword represents God. It shows that God is infinite, that God is without beginning or end. The two swords outside the circle are two Kirpans, the swords that Sikhs wear to defend the truth.

The children could study the symbols of other religions, finding out their significance and when and where they are used. This could lead to a wider investigation into the design and use of symbols. The children could design their own – to represent the class, the school, their family or other group they belong to.

The Bright Weather Festival

Ch'ing means clear and *ming* means bright, and Ch'ing-ming signifies weather suitable for going out into the countryside. Appropriately, the Ch'ing-ming Festival took place at the end of April or the beginning of May. It was the occasion chosen to carry out the annual family pilgrimage to the ancestral tombs.

Preparations began about ten days beforehand. First one of the elders bought many large sheets of coloured paper, which the ladies made into *Fen-piao*, 'grave banners'. They cut the paper into strips and wound the strips round a stick, changing the colour frequently. At the top they fixed a long pennon of paper which waved in the wind when the stick was set up on the tomb, indicating that descendants of the deceased had visited the spot. Fresh flowers were never placed on the tombs, and banners were only placed there once a year.

Like other young people of my family I went on my first pilgrimage at about the age of twelve, and, like them I am sure, my first impressions will always be vivid in my memory. My grandparents being unable to go, my third great-uncle took charge of the party. Not all the elders could leave home, and the aunts could not walk the distance on their small feet.

It was a lovely day, neither hot nor cold. The sun shone brightly, with intermittent drizzling showers. All the hills were green. The fields were planted with *yiu-tsai*, a plant with a group of tiny yellow flowers at the top of each stem; whole stretches of the countryside were carpeted with yellow. In some fields the young sprouts of wheat and rice were showing. The figures of farmers could be seen here and there; some were still sowing, some leading the buffalo out to plough, some singing *shan-ke* (hill songs) with a long-drawn intonation while they worked. This and the songs of the birds were the only sounds to be heard. In the quiet we could even hear the tiny hissing of the mild wind in the leaves and grasses. Nearly every hut or cottage we passed had some apricot or peach trees in bloom, and by the streams the willows were all fresh in their new green robes.

I was allowed to sit in the third great-uncle's sedan chair now and then when he wanted to walk for a change. But actually he told us so many stories of the countryside and pointed out so many interesting trees and herbs that I forgot to be tired . . .

The tombs which our group was going to visit were scattered on two hills. One of the tombs held the ancestor who had first moved our family from Northern China to Kiu-kiang. We youngsters busily unpacked the banners and dishes. We set a few banners on this tomb first and laid the dishes before it. Then we burnt incense and each of us in order of age knelt before the tomb. On one side was a stone tablet with the name of the dead and the dates of his birth and death, together with those of his wife; also a very brief account of how he had moved the family. Then we proceeded to the other tombs. My mother's was on the other hill. Father took my brother and sister and me to it while the rest of the group rested in a cottage. On the way I asked why we had not come to mother's tomb first. Father explained that the older ancestor had to be honoured first.

Farther down the slope of the hills were masses of wild azaleas, and the contrast of deep red and green made a beautiful picture. Father seemed very pleased with the scenery but he sighed deeply at times. After burning incense and letting off crackers Father bowed to the tomb three times, but we youngsters, the children of the deceased, knelt down and bowed our heads to the ground three times. Father did not speak except to tell us to read the inscription on the tombstone tablet. We were all silent for a while.

Presently we returned to the cottage. It was the duty of the people who occupied it to tend our tombs. My third great-uncle gave them renewed instructions and Father added a special word about Mother's tomb. Before leaving we picked a few branches of pine, peach and willow as well as a few azaleas to indicate that our ancestors would protect us and keep us as fresh and pure as these branches, which were, at the same time, tokens of spring to take back home.

Chiang Yee
from A Chinese childhood

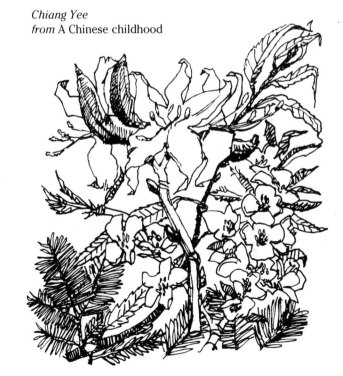

PASSOVER

For many Jews Passover is the big festival of the year, lasting seven or eight days. It has no fixed date, but it does occur in springtime and is sometimes known as the Festival of Spring. Its roots probably go back to two ancient spring festivals. Some of the early Jews were nomadic shepherds and, at the time the new lambs and goats were being born, each family or group would sacrifice one as a gift for their God. The tent posts were daubed with blood as a protection against evil. Other, more settled, Jews had a 'Feast of unleavened bread' to celebrate the barley harvest, when all sour doughs had to be destroyed, and a communal sacrifice was made of the new season's barley at the temple. Passover now combines elements of these two. There are services in the synagogue, but is primarily a family ceremony in remembrance of the time the Jews escaped from slavery in Egypt. It symbolises the Jewish struggle towards freedom, and also indicates hope for a world of peace and plenty for all.

First the whole house is cleaned thoroughly and all yeast and unleavened bread disposed of. Family and friends gather, traditionally wearing new clothes, and the table is set for the special Seder meal, a mixture of service, history lesson and family meal. There are candles on the table, a wine glass for everyone and an extra place for an unexpected visitor.

The meal itself consists of symbolic foods and, as the evening progresses, the youngest child asks certain questions related to the food. As the father answers, the story of the first Passover is recounted. Parsley is a symbol of spring, and it is dipped in salt water in remembrance of the tears of the Jewish slaves in Egypt and of the Red Sea that parted for them when they left. Bitter herbs, usually horseradish, are a reminder of the bitter time the Jews had in Egypt. They are dipped in a sweet paste, called Charoset, a symbol of the clay bricks the Hebrews had to make for the Pharaohs. The sweetness stands for God's kindness to the Jews even in their slavery. A roasted lamb bone suggests the lambs which were killed the night before the escape. The blood was smeared on the doorposts so that the Angel of Death would pass over the house. The family eats matzos (unleavened bread) because on the night of the exodus there was no time to let the dough rise. A cooked egg is another reminder of spring. A glass of wine is poured for Elijah, and the door left open. The evening ends with prayers and songs.

The Seder meal

Children can research in more detail the meaning of the various components of the Seder meal. There are a number of suitable books, including *Passover* by Lynne Scholefield in the Religious and Moral Education Press 'Living festivals' series and *Sam's Passover* by Lynne Hannigan in the A & C Black 'Celebrations' series. A model could be made of the Seder plate and the special food, using clay or papier mâché. Children could go on to find out about different types of unleavened bread, and perhaps try making some to see how they compare with ordinary bread.

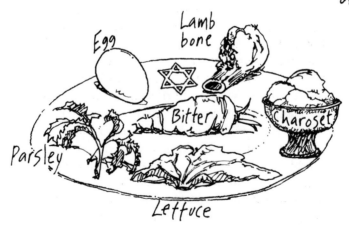

Retelling the Exodus story

The story of the Jewish slaves and the escape from Egypt is an exciting one. If you read it from Exodus, Chapter 12 in the Old Testament children could rewrite or retell it in modern language. It is also very suitable for acting, with both crowd and group scenes and plenty of action. The children could make it into a play, to be performed perhaps for an assembly. This could involve making scenery, costumes and props. Perhaps it could be video-recorded.

The story could also be told through a pictorial frieze, showing the different plagues and the stages of the exodus.

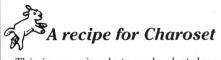
A recipe for Charoset

This is very simple to make, but does require fine chopping. A spring-action chopper where the blades are enclosed would obviously be safer and easier for classroom use than sharp knifes. The recipe should really be made with sweet wine, but for school use you can substitute grape juice.

These quantities will make enough for 30 children each to have a good dessertspoonful to taste.

You could use it with other foods to conduct food tasting tests, and lead onto research into the taste buds.

Utensils

safety chopper
chopping board
weighing scales
measuring jug
5 ml measuring spoon
bowl for mixing

Ingredients

400 g apples
100 g walnuts or blanched almonds
100g raisins
5 ml (1 teaspoon) ground cinnamon
100-150 ml grape juice

What to do

1 Peel the apples, cut in quarters, remove the core. Chop the apple finely.
2 Chop the nuts.
3 Mix apples, nuts, raisins and cinnamon with enough of the grape juice to make a paste.

An overcrowded house

In the entrance hall of my grandmother's flat, there was a cupboard set so high up in the wall that only a tall person standing on a chair could open it. Luckily, my grandmother needed what was kept up there once a year only, so it had to be reached on two occasions: once to bring out the Passover dishes ready for the Festival every spring, and the second time to put them all away for another twelve months. My tallest cousin, Arieh, was always the person who had to stand on the chair and pass down dishes and cups and plates, knives and forks and pots and pans and glasses to my grandmother and me, waiting to carry them to the kitchen.

At Passover time, all the ordinary dishes were put away and the whole flat was cleaned from top to bottom. Not a single crumb was allowed to lurk forgotten in a corner. Holes in the wall had to be plastered over. Sometimes, my grandmother decided that this or that room needed whitewashing, and she would pile all the furniture into the middle of the room for a day, and cover it with sheets, and then slap a thick, white sloppy brush up and down the walls.

'Why do you have the best things hidden away in the cupboard all the time?' I asked my grandmother. 'Why are they only allowed down into the house for a week?'

'Because it's a special celebration,' said my grandmother. 'It's to celebrate the escape of the Jews from their captivity in Egypt. We will read the whole story again, on the night of the First Seder.' For the Seder the door between the dining room and the room where the long blue sofa was, was folded back and the table was pulled out to its full length. More than twenty people would sit around it for the Passover meal, eating matzos and bitter herbs and drinking sweet wine, and telling the story of the Plagues that God sent down to the land of Egypt. In the Hagadah, the book we looked at as the meal continued, there were coloured drawings of the Plagues: frogs, locusts, boils, and a very frightening picture showing a dead child covered in blood and representing the Death of the Firstborn. There was also a picture of Moses parting the Red Sea, with high, blue waves towering above the heads of the Israelites like walls of sapphire. We sang songs, and waited up till late at night to see whether this year, the prophet Elijah would come and drink the glass of wine my grandmother always put out for him. At the end of the meal, my cousins and I would run all over the flat searching for the Afikoman. This was half a matzo wrapped in a napkin, which my grandmother hid like a treasure. Whoever found it won a small prize: an apple or a square of chocolate. There were so many cousins rushing about that I never managed to find the Afikoman, but my grandmother gave us all apples and chocolate too, so I didn't mind.

'It's not very fair for the winner, though,' I said to my grandmother. 'It makes winning less special.'

'Nonsense,' said my grandmother. 'Finding the Afikoman is an honour and it brings good luck. And looking all over the place is fun, too.'

In spite of the special dishes, and the book with pictures of the Plagues, in spite of the sips of sweet wine and the brown-freckled matzos which tasted so delicious with strawberry jam on them, I was always quite glad when the festival was over and the visitors went home. Then I could have my grandmother to myself again and she could tell me stories.

Adele Geras

Carnival

Carnival, Mas carnival
Mas carnival, Mas carnival.

Walk out into the street,
The music grabs your feet.
Big parade, music played,
To the conga beat.
Makes you dance, makes you sway,
Makes you feel on holiday, when it's –
    Carnival, Mas carnival . . .

No matter where you are,
It's time for Mardi Gras.
Have some fun, winter's done,
Summer can't be far.
So let's dance, and let's sway,
And let's have a holiday, now it's –
    Carnival, Mas carnival . . .

Pushing through the press
Nobody can guess
Who you are behind your mask
Wearing fancy dress.
So you dance, and you sway,
And enjoy the holiday, now it's –
    Carnival, Mas carnival . . .

Lanterns burning bright
Shining in the night,
Candles flicker, torches blaze,
Everywhere there's light.
And we dance, and we sway,
And enjoy our holiday, when it's –
    Carnival, Mas carnival . . .

Words and music by David Moses

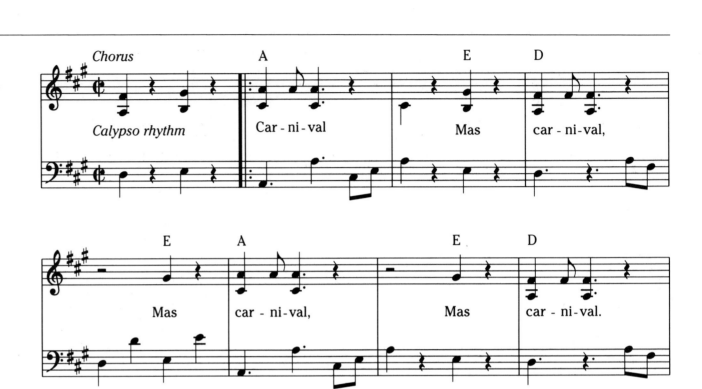

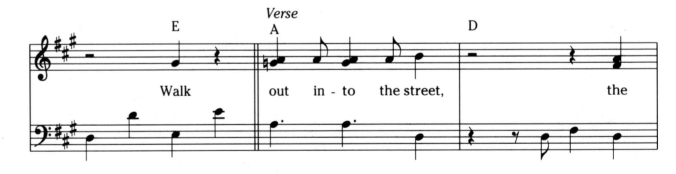

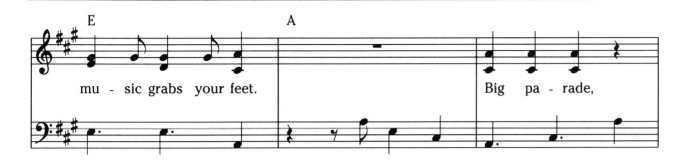

mu - sic grabs your feet. Big pa - rade,

mu - sic played, to the con - ga beat. Makes you dance, makes you

sway, Makes you feel on ho - li - day, when it's

To end, repeat the chorus ad lib and fade.

CARNIVAL

The word 'carnival' comes from an old Latin phrase *carnem levare*, which means 'to take away meat'. In Christian countries it has become associated with the preparations for Lent. Lent is the period of self-denial which starts on Ash Wednesday and leads up to Easter. The main events of carnival usually happen on Shrove Tuesday. In some countries this is known as Mardi Gras – 'Fat Tuesday'. It was the day when rich food, like eggs, would be used up in dishes like pancakes, for example.

Carnival is a time for dressing up in strange and elaborate masks and costumes and a time for music and dancing. As the concept of carnival spread across the world, local traditions, cultures and music were absorbed. Carnival was – and is – forever changing and developing from the original European form.

In Europe too there are number of different ancient traditions. In some places mock battles were fought between actors representing summer and winter. Summer always won. This was to ensure the coming of spring, a period of regeneration, and a good harvest.

Many carnivals have their own traditional characters, for example, Moco Jumbie from Trinidad and Tobago and King Carnival from Europe.

Mardi Gras was introduced to New Orleans, USA, by the French Colonialists and is a mixture of European and South American Indian influences. The carnivals of Rio de Janeiro and the Caribbean have very strong African influences.

Music and dancing play a very big part in carnival. There are many competitions to see which group is the best band or has the best dancers. Rehearsals for the next carnival start immediately the current one is over. There is often great rivalry and secrecy between competing groups. The music of New Orleans is jazz; in the Caribbean it is calypso and in Rio it is samba.

Linking activities

A spring festival

There is so much to celebrate in spring – the warmer weather, the longer days, the birth of animals and birds, the bursting forth of plants, buds and blossom. Your class or school could devise their own spring festival, perhaps just one assembly, or possibly a much grander occasion.

Parades are often a central part of a spring celebration, whether it is a May Day parade (see page 52), an Easter parade (page 64) or a carnival (page 74). You could organise your own, perhaps on a theme which is special to your school or local area and featuring famous local characters or stories. Or it could be on the theme of spring itself, or on the triumph of good over evil. A parade would provide lots of opportunities for art and craft in the making of hats, costumes, masks and banners; for music-making; and for dancing.

A school garden

The best way for children to learn about the life cycles of plants, insects and other creatures, and to appreciate the miracle of the yearly rebirth, is for them to experience it at first hand. A school garden is an ideal resource. A wonderful book to introduce the idea to children is *Our hidden garden*, by Beverley Birch with photographs by Nick Birch, published by Hamish Hamilton/Evans. It celebrates the story of a luxuriant garden in an inner-city infants' school. There are a number of organisations and books which can help with setting up a school garden, including *Gardening for wildlife*, available from The Urban Trust, Unit 213, Jubilee Trades Centre, 130 Pershore Street, Birmingham B5 6ND. Learning Through Landscapes Trust is another useful organisation offering a variety of materials and advice. They are at: Third Floor, Southside Offices, The Law Courts, Winchester, Hants SO23 9DL. If you are thinking of setting up a new garden, the children can be involved right from initial planning through to the planting out and after-care.

If a garden is not possible, you could plant some tubs or window boxes. In one infants' school the children nurtured some hollyhocks growing in a very narrow border along a wall, saved and stored the seeds, packaged them in packets which they had designed and made themselves and sold them at the school Christmas Fair. The money raised bought other seeds the following spring.

 **A three-dimensional spring mural**

This is by no means a new idea, but a spring mural can involve far more arts and crafts than tissue paper blossoms and cotton wool lambs. One part could depict the life cycle of frogs or toads. You could use plastic bubble packaging with black dots stuck on to them for the spawn and black-eyed beans in scrunched-up clingfilm for the nearly-hatched tadpoles. The developing frogs can be made from clay or other modelling material, or from cloth, cut out, sewn and stuffed. Try to get a range of models from the stage where the back legs have appeared to the fully grown frog.

Many books on origami have frogs in them, so some children might like to try that.

Caterpillars can easily be made from painted egg cartons or stuffed old tights, socks or stockings and very effective butterflies and moths can be made from wire coat hangers covered with light material and decorated. You could also try ink blot butterflies, where paint or ink is spattered on one half of a sheet of paper. The paper is then folded to obtain a mirror image, and the shape of a butterfly cut out.

Children's shape poems (see page 43) could be incorporated as part of the illustration – instead of a row of plants growing there could be a row of poems, or a tree-shaped poem.

 Myths and stories

More than any other season, spring has always had mystical significance. Many of the stories, poems and accounts of festivals in this book show how spring is associated with the triumph of good over evil, with fertility, rebirth and making a new start. You can use the material in this book as a way of introducing other myths, whether or not they are connected with spring.

Books containing creation stories from around the world include: *Creation stories* retold by Jon Mayled, published by Wayland and *Worlds of difference* by Martin Palmer and Esther Bisset, published by WWF/Blackie.

Children could invent their own creation stories, either for the world as a whole (see *The Trimurti*, page 20), for particular features (*The rainbow*, page 25) or animals (*Wumbulgul*, page 16) or plants (*A wondrous thing*, page 40).

Many religions have a god of thunder (see *The rainbow*, page 25). Encourage children to look up the various names for this god in books of Greek, Norse and Roman myths and read their stories.

The Greek myth about Echo could tie in with investigations into bats and sonar devices (see page 35) and work on hibernation could include reading stories about people who have slept for a long time, such as Sleeping Beauty and Rip Van Winkle. Ask the children to imagine what the world would be like if they woke up after sleeping for many years. They could write a story about it, either individually or as a group, and perhaps dramatise it.

A caterpillar is described as 'an eating machine' (page 34) and The Voracious Vacuum Cleaner (page 48) is certainly another. The children might know of more stories about creatures with huge appetites. They could invent their own stories about an eating machine and write an adventure story.

Index

Poems

titles and *first lines*

Stories

Songs

titles and *first lines*

Acknowledgments

The following have kindly granted their permission for the reprinting of copyright words and music:

Blackie Children's Books for **Butterfly** from *Sources* by Jean Kenward.

The Bodley Head for **The Easter Hare** from *To Read and to Tell* by Norah Montgomerie; **The first day** from *A Song of Sunlight* by Phoebe Hesketh; **All Fools' Day** from *I Din Do Nuttin* by John Agard.

Ann Bonner for **April 1st**.

Cambridge University Press for **Climbing to Heaven** from *Legends of Earth, Air, Fire & Water* by Eric and Tessa Hadley.

Jonathan Cape Ltd for **The last slice of rainbow** by Joan Aitken.

Laura Cecil Literary Agency for **The Voracious Vacuum Cleaner** from *Stuff and Nonsense* edited by Laura Cecil; **The Overcrowded House** from *My Grandmother's Stories* by Adèle Geras.

Chiang Chien-Fei for **The Bright Weather Festival** from *A Chinese Childhood* by Chiang Yee.

The Literary Executor of Leonard Clark for **New Baby** and **Miracle** by Leonard Clark.

Veronica Clark for **Easter round**.

Pie Corbett for **Coming out of hibernation**.

Niki Davies for **April fool**, **Could this be a sign?** **Spring cleaning rap**.

Aileen Fisher for **The Seed** from *Up the Windy Hill* by Aileen Fisher.

George Allen & Unwin, now Unwin Hyman of HarperCollins Publishers Limited (for the World excluding USA), and Alfred A. Knopf Inc. (for the USA) for **Clearing at Dawn** from *Translations from the Chinese* by Arthur Waley, translator. Copyright 1919 and renewed 1947 by Arthur Waley. Reprinted by permission.

Ginn & Company Ltd for *The rainbow* from *Tales from South East Asia* by Beulah Candappa.

HarperCollins Publishers Limited for **Hare and the Easter egg** by Alison Uttley.

HarperCollins Publishers NY Inc for **The last slice of rainbow** by Joan Aitken.

Hodder & Stoughton Limited for **A wondrous thing** from *Velvet Paws and Whiskers* compiled by Jean Chapman.

Libby Houston for **black dot**.

Michael Joseph for **For Easter** and **For a dance** from *Silver, Sand and Snow* by Eleanor Farjeon.

Sandra Kerr for **New life beginning**.

James Kirkup for **The Doll Festival**.

The Literary Trustees of Walter de la Mare and their representative The Society of Authors for **Seeds** by Walter de la Mare.

The Macmillan Company of Australia Pty Ltd for **The universal egg** from *Creation Stories* retold by Maureen Stewart.

John Travers Moore for **Springburst** from *There's Motion Everywhere* by John Travers Moore. Copyright 1970 by John Travers Moore and published by the Houghton Mifflin Co.

Brian Moses for **Spring in the city**.

David Moses for **Carnival**, and **I'm a chick I am**.

Oxford University Press for **Winter's end**. Reprinted from *The Whole World Storybook* by Marcus Crouch (1983). © Marcus Crouch 1983. Used by permission of Oxford University Press.

Pavilion Books Ltd for **Holi – Festival of Spring** from *Seasons of Splendour* by Madhur Jaffrey. Reprinted by permission.

Penguin Books Ltd for **The swallows' creation** by Tansy Hutchinson from *Words on Water*, Various.

Copyright © Tansy Hutchinson 1987. Reprinted by permission of Penguin Books Ltd.

The Peters Fraser & Dunlop Group Ltd for **The fight of the year** from *You Tell Me* by Roger McGough, published by Viking Kestrel; **Over** and **A poem with knickers in it** from *Nailing the Shadow* by Roger McGough, published by Jonathan Cape.

Harriet Powell for **Spring changes**.

Irene Rawnsley for **Holi**.

Matt Simpson for **There goes Winter** and **Spring**.

Tamar Swade for **Spring is here**.

Syndication International (1986) Ltd for **The catkin** by Lindsay Holley © Daily Mirror Children's Literary Competition 1974.

Tro Essex Music Ltd and Schroder Music Co. for **Star flower** by Malvina Reynolds, © 1961 Schroder Music Co. All rights for British Commonwealth (excluding Canada), Republics of Ireland and South Africa controlled by Tro-Essex Music Ltd. International copyright secured. All rights for USA and Canada controlled by Schroder Music Co. All rights reserved. Used by permission.

Walker Books for **Lavinia Bat** from *Ponders* by Russell Hoban; **At long last, spring has arrived** and **I planted some seeds** by Colin McNaughton from *There's an awful lot of weirdos in our Neighbourhood*.

Wayland (Publishers) Limited for **The Trimurti** from *Creation Stories* retold by Jon Mayled. Reproduced with the kind permission of Wayland (Publishers) Limited, 61 Western Road, Hove, East Sussex BN3 1JD.